Michael has been on leave from his job as an enforcer since he was stabbed while on a mission. He feels ready to get back to work, but Jared, the Whitedell pride doctor, won't let him. He's relieved when he and two of his team members are sent on a short, easy mission—and so is everyone else in the pride, because he's whined about being bored for weeks. But the mission isn't as easy as Michael had thought it would be, and the biggest surprise for him is smelling his mate in the house he's supposed to check.

Cooper has been stuck in the Green Hill pride mansion for close to fifteen years. His alpha is obsessed with keeping the pride members there since several of them left, and Cooper is the one paying the highest price. He's the pride's slave, and he's beaten regularly.

But when he smells his mate at the front door, he knows things are about to change.

Michael needs to get his mate out of that house. Cooper is stronger than most people give him credit for, and he manages to escape on his own. They both know Alpha Carter isn't going to take it kindly, though. Bonding will make sure Cooper isn't forced to go back, but will Alpha Carter stop and acknowledge it, or will they have to find another way to keep Cooper in Whitedell?

Michael
Copyright © 2019 Catherine Lievens
ISBN: 978-1-4874-2419-0
Cover art by Angela Waters

Published by eXtasy Books Inc or
Devine Destinies, an imprint of eXtasy Books Inc

Look for us online at:
www.eXtasybooks.com or www.devinedestinies.com

MICHAEL
COUNCIL ENFORCERS BOOK 19

BY

CATHERINE LIEVENS

CHAPTER ONE

"You're pouting. It looks good on you, but you've also been bitching almost non-stop, and no one likes that."

Michael glared at Nysys. "You'd be bitching too in my place."

Nysys shrugged. "I don't know. A forced vacation? Why are your panties in a twist? I'd be all over that."

Michael was pretty sure that was true, and that he should be using this time to relax, maybe watch the TV shows he never had time for. He hated not being able to work, though, especially when it was for something as stupid as being wounded on the job. "I'm healed. Hell, I was healed as soon as I walked through the door. I can go back to work."

Nysys patted Michael's thigh. "I'm sure you were, but there has to be a reason you haven't been cleared yet. Maybe Jared wants to make sure you don't have any lingering effects due to the wounds? Physical and mental?"

Michael glared harder. "I'm not going crazy."

Nysys rolled his eyes. "Who said you were going crazy?"

"And it wasn't the first time I was wounded while on a mission." Although it *was* the first time most of the team had needed to leave someone behind because it had been safer for everyone. Michael didn't blame them. Why would he? They'd all done their jobs, and everything had been all right. Even Sasha and Hunter had come back in one piece. Michael had been the worst one off, with his two knife wounds, but Nysys had shimmered him right into the infirmary, and he'd been taken care of right away.

So why hadn't he been cleared for work yet? It had been weeks. He was healed. He felt good. He *wanted* to get back to work.

"I'm bored," he whined.

Nysys huffed and got up. "I can't watch TV with you when you're like this. I can't even *hear* the TV over your whining."

"Benji hasn't complained," Michael pointed out, slightly wounded. His brother was curled up next to him and had stayed out of the conversation until now.

"That's because he *has* to stick with you. You're his brother." Nysys wiggled his fingers. "But I'm going. I'm sure I can find something more interesting to do than listen to you whine."

"Good riddance," Michael muttered as Nysys walked away.

Benjamin sighed. "You know, he's not wrong."

Michael's chest tightened. "What, you stick around only because we're related?"

Benjamin rolled his eyes. "No. I stick around because I love you and I know how frustrated you are. I even understand it, in a way. You love your job, and you hate to be on the sidelines." His voice went softer. "And you still want to prove to our father that you can do this, even though you two haven't talked since you moved to Whitedell. It's been almost fifteen years, Michael. You have to let go of that."

"I don't care about him." And it was true. If anything, he was glad his parents had brought him along when they'd come to Whitedell for Benjamin. It had given him a chance to see there could be more for him than the life they'd planned for him, and he'd grabbed the chance with both hands.

He hadn't yet let go. He loved his job. He loved feeling like he mattered, like what he did changed things for people. He couldn't help wondering if people were getting hurt because he hadn't been cleared for missions. Of course, he knew there were plenty of other enforcers, but there were also plenty of bad guys, even though the number of shifters and paranormal creatures in the world was nowhere near to the number of humans.

"Why don't you go talk to Sarah or Emerson?"

"I already talked to Sarah. She said she couldn't do anything. She's not the one in charge of the enforcers, and she's not the one who decides who does what."

"What about Emerson?"

Michael hadn't talked to the local head of the enforcers because he already knew the answer he'd get, but maybe it was worth a try. He'd been home for two weeks already, and he was *fine*. "Not yet."

"Why don't you go? The worst he can do is tell you no. That wouldn't be great for those of us who have to spend time with you, but at least you'd know. You can even ask him why he's not sending you and your team out right now. Maybe having an answer will help you deal with it."

Michael wasn't sure about that, but Benjamin was right. At least he'd know why, and he could try to change his mind and convince him he could be sent back to work.

Michael loved living in Whitedell. He loved spending time with friends he had outside of the team and his brother. He didn't get to do it often. But two weeks was too much. It wasn't even that he wanted to go who knew where. He just needed something to do. He'd had enough of reading books and watching stupid TV shows.

He kissed his brother's forehead and got up. "Thanks."

Benjamin smiled. "What for?"

"For listening to me bitch for the past two weeks."

"Like Nysys said, you're my brother. I kind of had to."

Michael laughed. "Whatever. Let's just hope Emerson has something for me to do." The best would be for the team to be sent out, but Michael would accept anything, even if it meant babysitting the new recruits or whatever. As long as he wasn't forced to spend one more minute on the couch or in his room, he'd be fine.

He found Emerson in his office. He knocked, and when Emerson told him to come in, he did, but he almost backed out as soon as he saw that Dominic was there, too.

"What's wrong, Michael?" Dominic asked.

"Nothing. Sorry for interrupting. I'll come back later."

"You're not interrupting. We were having a chat. Do you need me to go?"

Michael sighed. He wanted to say yes, but it wasn't like Emerson wouldn't talk to Dominic about this anyway. Michael was both an enforcer and a pride member, after all.

He closed the door behind himself and hovered there, Emerson and Dominic staring at him. He shuffled and decided he might as well get straight to the point. "I'd like to go back to work. I've been home for two weeks now, and I was healed as soon as I got back. I'm perfectly fine."

Emerson leaned back in his chair. "Are you sure about that?"

"Of course I am. I wouldn't be here otherwise."

"*Or* you'd be here anyway because you can't stand hanging around the house." He sighed. "I need to talk to Jared first. He's the reason you're still here, and I can't send you anywhere until I have his go-ahead."

Michael groaned. As a pride member, it was Jared who took care of him, not the healer in charge of the enforcers. It would no doubt have been easier to be sent back to work if Michael hadn't had Jared on his case. "I can talk to him," he said.

Emerson grinned. "I don't think so. *I'll* talk to him and ask him what he thinks about you going back to work."

"He's never going to say yes."

"I don't know. Like you said, you've been home for two weeks. You're probably fine."

"I am."

"I still need Jared to tell me you're okay to get back to work. He's your doctor. But I promise I'll talk to him today and let you know by the end of the day, okay?"

"But I—"

"It's all I can do."

Dominic cleared his throat. "I'm sure your brother won't mind having to listen to you complain a few more days."

Michael glared at him. He wouldn't have dared if he'd only been an enforcer, but he'd lived with the pride for almost fifteen years, and even though Dominic was the alpha, he was family, much more so than Michael's parents had ever been. "You're not funny. I know you think you are, but you're not."

"No? I could try some of my dad jokes."

"Please, no. That would be worse than having to watch daytime television. I'm going." He looked at Emerson. "By the end of the day?"

"Promise."

It wasn't what Michael had hoped for, but it was better than he'd expected. He could deal with waiting a few more hours—and hopefully, that was all the time he'd still have to wait. He wasn't sure what he'd do if Emerson told him he had to stay put. Go crazy, probably.

****

Cooper peeked into the bedroom. It was empty, and he knew he wouldn't get a better opportunity than this one.

He snuck in.

The room was a mess, but then, it always was in the

morning. It made Cooper wonder what Alpha Carter did every night with his wife. He didn't want to know, though, not really. The last thing he needed was to have to imagine the asshole in bed hurting her.

Because Cooper was sure he did. Alpha Carter hurt everyone, always. It didn't matter that the poor woman was his third wife and that he'd pushed the first to divorce, and the second to suicide. It didn't matter that his third wife had just had a baby. Alpha Carter was trying to repopulate the pride, and he wouldn't stop for anything or anyone.

Cooper picked up the dirty laundry, wrinkling his nose. He didn't want to think about what the stains on them were from, either. At least he wouldn't have to wash them.

A cry from the bathroom startled him, and he dropped Alpha Carter's underwear. He scowled at the dirty fabric and hesitated. He didn't have a way to know who was in the bathroom, but since Alpha Carter spent most of his days in his office, he thought it was probably his wife — Annabelle — and their new baby. She was a nice woman, but she kept her distance from him. He understood why, and he didn't care much. He didn't care about anyone in the pride, not now that Lenny and Scott had left.

They hadn't even been friends, but they'd been the only ones who'd ever treated Cooper like he was human, like the fact that he was gay didn't make him less of a man or a person. Of course, that was probably because they were gay, too, and he wished they'd thought of him when they'd left the pride. Why should they have, though? They probably hadn't thought twice about him since they'd left Green Hill. But he thought about them often. He thought about the chances they had, the possibility of a new life — something Cooper would never have.

He wasn't even allowed to leave pride territory. He knew a way out, of course, but what would he find out there if he did leave? He didn't have friends, didn't know anyone out-side the pride. He didn't know how to contact Lenny and Scott or where to find them. He didn't have a cent, so he would never be able to survive on his own. He could shift and live in his tiger form, but that wasn't what he wanted.

He wanted to be free. He wanted to be able to find a place where he'd belong, to find love and happiness. He'd never get that if he stayed, but what were the chances he would if he left? Besides, Alpha Carter would never let him go far. He might be able to sneak out, but the alpha was obsessive. He wanted to keep all his pride members in sight at all times, which was why no one but he and his beta were allowed to leave pride territory.

It was a prison, and Cooper hated thinking that he'd have to spend the rest of his life stuck there. He was used as a slave by the pride. He was considered the lowest member because he couldn't get married and have children, not from a woman anyway.

"Please, please, stop crying," Annabelle begged from the bathroom.

Cooper sighed. Alpha Carter wouldn't be happy if he found out Cooper had taken care of his son. Cooper often wondered if Alpha Carter thought being gay was catching or something. He sure behaved like he did. Still, Cooper went to knock on the bathroom door. "Annabelle?" he asked, keeping his voice soft and gentle. He'd already heard Alpha Carter berate her too many times about how she was with the baby.

"Coo—Cooper?"

"It's me."

The door opened. There was a bruise on Annabelle's cheek, and she looked like she'd been crying. She was hold-ing her baby, and he was still crying. "I can't make him stop," she said.

She was painfully young, around twenty if Cooper remembered right. Her parents had negotiated her marriage to
Alpha Carter, and she'd gotten the short straw. She was in
over her head, and Cooper didn't know how to help her.
"He's not going to be happy if he hears the baby," he said
even though they both already knew that.

"I know, but I can't make him stop."

Cooper looked back at the bedroom door. Dammit. He
didn't want to do this. He also didn't want Alpha Carter to
beat Annabelle again, though. "Give him to me."

Her eyes widened. "What?"

"I have experience with babies." Even though he
shouldn't, since the alpha didn't want him to touch them, it
didn't mean the other pride members had the same problem,
though, and he'd often babysat kids.

"But . . ."

"I know. He's in his office right now. Come on. You need
to clean yourself up. You know he's going to get angry if he
finds you still wearing your pajamas and with your hair all
over the place."

Annabelle bit her lower lip. Cooper huffed.

"Look, I want to help you. I can go if you'd rather do this
on your own, though." She was a victim, but he had to think
of himself, and he'd be the one to get beaten if she didn't
hurry up.

She finally handed him the baby. "Thank you."

"Did you feed him?"

"Yes. Just now."

"Good. Take a shower. I'll take care of him."

Cooper held the baby close and stepped away from the
bathroom door. He gently patted the baby's back and
hummed to him as he paced the bedroom length. He needed
to continue cleaning before Alpha Carter decided he needed
something from the bedroom.

When the bedroom door opened, Cooper closed his eyes. He already knew he was in trouble, even though he'd gotten the baby to stop crying.

"What the fuck is going on here? Why are you holding my son?" Alpha Carter's voice boomed.

The baby startled awake and started crying right away. Cooper forced himself to face the alpha, but he didn't look him in the eyes. "I'm sorry. Your wife needed a moment to shower."

"I don't care what Annabelle needed. You can't touch my son."

Cooper wasn't about to hand him to Alpha Carter or to put the month-old baby on the floor. "I apologize, Alpha. I was trying to help, and I do have to obey your wife's orders." He hated to push Annabelle under the bus that way, but he'd been Alpha Carter's punching bag for decades, and he knew what his fists would feel like.

"Annabelle!" Alpha Carter yelled.

The baby cried harder. Annabelle came out of the bathroom. She was dressed, thankfully, even though her hair was still damp. Her eyes were wide, and she rushed to Cooper, snatching the baby. They both knew what was coming, for both of them, although the alpha would probably wait for tonight to punish his wife.

The hit came almost too soon, just as the baby got into his mother's arms. Cooper's head snapped back, and he stumbled. He fell when the second hit got him in the stomach, and he curled up, wondering if the alpha was going to stop at a few slaps and punches, or if this was going to be one of his longer punishments.

Alpha Carter grabbed Cooper's long hair and used it to pull his head up. It hurt, and Cooper hoped he wouldn't end up half bald by the time this was over. "You *never* touch my children. Do you hear me?" the alpha spat through gritted teeth.

Cooper swallowed. "Yes, Alpha." He wanted to tell Alpha Carter to fuck off, but he liked being alive and being able to move. He would already be in plenty of pain after what had just happened. Things weren't going to get better if he got mouthy. He knew that from experience.

Alpha Carter pushed Cooper away. The back of Cooper's head hit the floor and he groaned, pain exploding in his head, bright and sharp and overwhelming.

"I'll take care of you tonight," Alpha Carter said to his wife.

Cooper pressed his cheek against the floor. He had to get up, but there was no way he'd do that while Alpha Carter was in the room. It would only make him more of a target.

He wanted this to end. He *needed* this to end. If only he knew how to make that happen.

****

Michael looked at the scar on his shoulder and pressed a fingertip against it. It didn't even hurt anymore, so why was he stuck in Whitedell?

"Stop doing that," Hunter told him. He poked Michael's thigh with his socked foot.

Michael wrinkled his nose and shuffled away. "I'm not doing anything."

"You're touching your wound."

"It's not a wound anymore. It's a scar. And shouldn't you be in Gillham with Sasha?"

"He had to work today. I'm going back later tonight unless we're sent out."

Michael sighed. "Do you think we will be?"

Hunter's pitying gaze told Michael all he needed to know.

He sighed and let go of his t-shirt. "Who's taking you

back to Gillham?" Maybe he could tag along. It would be better than hanging around the mansion again.

"Pryderi."

Michael looked at the Nix. He was spread out on the other couch, his phone in his hand. He was staring at it, and Michael couldn't tell what he was doing. Reading, maybe? "Would you mind if I tagged along?" he asked.

Pryderi blinked. "What?"

"Tonight. You're taking Hunter to Gillham, right?"

"Yeah."

"Do you mind if I come along?"

"Of course not."

Pryderi looked distracted, and Michael frowned. "What's going on? You're never this quiet, and I feel like I haven't seen you enough lately. You're barely around."

To Michael's surprised, Pryderi's cheeks flushed. "I *am* around. I've just been busy."

"Busy? We're stuck here."

"That doesn't mean I don't have stuff to do. You've been spending time with your brother, right?"

"Of course."

"And I've been doing other stuff, running errands, things like that. Don't worry about me. I'm perfectly fine, and I'm enjoying the time we have to relax and do stuff."

"Stuff, huh?" Hunter asked. "And what kind of stuff do you have to do in Gillham?"

"See people. I have other friends, you know."

"Yeah? Is one of those friends a human bar owner?"

Michael arched a brow. "You mean Nate?"

Pryderi's cheeks went even redder. "I wasn't asking about him."

"You're sure about that? Because I think I've noticed you at the bar more often than I knew you were in town," Hunter said.

"Michael?"

Pryderi looked like he might kiss Dominic for interrupting the conversation. Michael, on the other hand, held his breath. He was about to find out if the team could be sent out on missions again.

He sat up. "Hey?"

Dominic smiled. "Do you want to go to my office? Emerson wanted to be the one telling you this, but he got a call, and he had to answer. I didn't want you to have to wait too long."

"It's fine here." It wasn't like Pryderi and Hunter wouldn't find out anyway if the team got called back.

"All right. Emerson and I talked to Jared, and while he agrees it's probably overkill, he wants you to take things slow."

Michael groaned. "Slow? I'm taking things so slowly that if I go any slower, I'll start going backward."

"That doesn't make sense," Hunter muttered.

Michael kicked him.

Dominic cleared his throat. "I said slow, not still. While Jared thinks we should wait to send you and the team out on a lengthy and complicated mission, he didn't have anything against finding you a calmer job to do, especially since part of the team is still busy with their things."

Michael wasn't sure he liked the sound of this. "Calmer job?"

"The council has a list of packs, prides, and other shifter and paranormal groups that isolated themselves and aren't answering calls or e-mails. We need someone to go over that list and visit them to make sure everything is fine."

Great, so Michael was going to have to play parent checking on their kid. It was better than nothing, though. He'd get to leave the mansion and do something. "What do you expect from those visits?"

Dominic sighed. "I wish I could say that having a pack dropping out of touch like this wasn't worrying, but most of the time, it is. Some of them do prefer to be on their own and live in the woods, especially Nix tribes, but a lot of the time, isolation hides abuse. Alphas tend to do that when they don't want anyone to notice how badly they treat their people, and the council cannot ignore that. We've been assigning enforcers to check in on them routinely, but there's a lot of work to do, and not enough enforcers to do it. That's why I'd be grateful if you accepted to do this."

"Of course I will." Michael didn't even have to think about it, especially not after what Dominic had said. He'd chosen to become an enforcer to help people, and that didn't always mean raiding drug dealers in the jungle. He could do it by finding out if people were abused and getting their alpha arrested.

"We don't want you to intervene, even if you do think something is wrong. I know your first instinct would be to do just that, but you'll be alone, and it's too dangerous."

"I'll go with him," Pryderi offered.

Dominic nodded. "Good. It would be better if you could find at least another person, but again, I don't want you to break into homes or push your way into territories. Go there, try to talk to the alpha and maybe to some of their people, then file a report. Take as many notes as you can, and if you think there's a problem, we can send a full team, maybe even you once Jared gives you the all-clear. Understood?"

Michael nodded. It made sense. He might be eager to get back to work, but he wasn't going to put himself and innocent people in danger just because he was itching to do more. He knew his job, and he was good at it.

Dominic's shoulders relaxed. "Thank you, Michael. I expected more of a fight, to be honest."

"I told you, I just want to do something. I'm feeling perfectly fine. So thank *you* for doing this."

"Why don't you come to my office? I'll give you the list so you can start working on it. And you and Pryderi should find another person to go with you. You can start tomorrow, so you should prepare everything today."

Michael was eager to get back into things, so he didn't mind starting today. "We'll ask the other team members who are around if they have anything to do." He already knew Hunter was out, and he didn't blame him. Once the team was put back on rotation, Hunter wouldn't have a lot of time to be with his mate, so he needed to take advantage of it now that he could visit Sasha as often as he wanted to.

Michael followed Dominic to his office and got the list from him, or one of the lists, anyway, since when Dominic opened the folder to take it out, Michael saw it was full of sheets of paper. Maybe it wasn't a bad thing that Jared hadn't yet cleared him for regular work. There apparently was a lot of this stuff to do and not enough people to do it.

Michael gave the list a quick read as he walked back to the living room in the enforcers' wings of the mansion. There were three prides, two packs, three Nix tribes, one sleuth, and even a wendigo tribe on it. Michael suspected that Dominic was right and that the Nix and the wendigo probably preferred to be on their own, but that didn't mean he wasn't going to check. As for the others, he was going to go in with his eyes open and suspecting there was foul play behind their isolation. There was no way all these people just liked being on their own in the woods.

Hunter was gone when Michael got back to the living room. He rolled his eyes. "He ran away, huh?"

Pryderi shrugged. "You knew he had plans."

"Weren't you supposed to shimmer him to Gillham?"

"I will, as soon as the two of us go over that list and we talk about it. Hunter's dick can wait another hour."

Michael flopped next to Pryderi. "Who do you think we can ask? Anyone from the team around?"

"How about Justin? I'm pretty sure he's been hiding out in his bedroom."

Justin was their werewolf, and while everyone loved him, he tended to want space to be on his own. He was the most recent team member, and Michael suspected he wasn't used to being accepted for who and what he was. "Sounds great. I'll go find him once you and Hunter are gone."

Michael had a plan, at last, and he couldn't wait to get back to work.

****

Cooper wiggled out of the window. He plastered his back against the wall and slid sideways, keeping his focus on his feet until he reached the edge of the roof. Then he turned, pressed one hand on the roof next to the trellis, and turned around. The trellis shook with every move he made, but he got to the ground safely, just like he always did when he snuck out of the house.

He pushed his hair away from his face and looked around, just in case, even though he knew people only rarely left the house. That was mostly because Alpha Carter had forbidden it, but Cooper was the only one who'd spent much time in the garden even before that.

He frowned at the state of his flowers. They were all dead by now, suffocated by wild grass and lack of care. He made his way on what had once been a path but was now little more than an overgrown graveled area and moved away from the house.

This was why he'd always enjoyed the garden. It was big, but not too big, and he'd found the hidden place when he was a kid and still allowed to run around. There hadn't been much to it back then, but he'd worked on it while he'd still been able to, and now it was a perfect hiding place.

It was tucked away to the side, near the fence that ran along the entire perimeter of pride territory. The trees and bushes were plentiful there, and Cooper had installed a small bench between them. The vegetation hid it, and the only way to see it was to walk in front of it. These days, he encouraged the bushes to grow in front of it. He hoped it would create a small enclave where he could spend time hiding from the world, or at least, from *his* world.

He didn't want to hide from what was outside the fence, but from what was inside of it.

He pushed the bushes to the side and slid onto the bench. The bushes didn't cover the entire bench, so Cooper made sure to move to the side that wasn't visible. He doubted anyone had noticed him leaving the house, or even that anyone had decided to do the same and sneak out. He knew other pride members didn't like what Alpha Carter was doing, but most of those who had a problem with him had slowly trickled out over the years, like Lenny and Scott. They were free now, and Cooper sometimes wondered if living in the forest in his tiger form wouldn't be better than the daily beatings he took.

He knew it would be.

He was inching closer and closer to making that decision and changing his life. He wasn't sure what held him back, but it was probably fear. He didn't care about leaving his parents behind—they'd never tried to defend him from Alpha Carter, and he didn't think they ever would. He didn't have siblings, something that made Alpha Carter angry with his family. No, Cooper wouldn't regret anything he'd leave behind.

But he was afraid. He was *terrified*. He had no way of knowing what he'd find when he left the pride. As bad as living there was, as much as he hated Alpha Carter and everyone else in the pride for not taking a stand against him, it was his home, and all he knew. Not being able to tell what would happen to him once he left it was what held him back, but he'd get over it soon. He knew it.

He sighed. He loved spending time outside, but he could never stay long, not when Alpha Carter might need him. The man wasn't predictable except in the way he'd make Cooper pay if he didn't find him when he needed him or when Cooper did something he didn't like. That happened all too often, and it was Cooper's fault. If only he could keep his mouth shut. But sometimes, the words got out of his mouth without him even thinking about it.

He got up and brushed his ass off. He looked around, and when he was satisfied he was alone, he snuck back to the house. He managed to get all the way to the trellis before getting caught, and he was glad he hadn't started climbing it, because that would have been a dead giveaway of how he'd left the house.

"What are you doing outside?" Beta Boyd asked, his voice harsh and cold. He was as bad as Alpha Carter, so Cooper didn't even try to mollify him.

"I wanted to check the flowers."

Beta Boyd snorted. "They've been dead for a long time."

"I couldn't have known that, since I haven't been allowed to leave the house in a long time."

Beta Boyd's eyes blazed with anger. "Mouthy, aren't you? Well, it's nothing Alpha Carter can't deal with." He grabbed Cooper's arm and dragged him toward the front door.

Cooper didn't protest and didn't try to fight his hold even though it hurt. It was nothing next to what awaited him, and it would only make Alpha Carter and Beta Boyd angrier.

Beta Boyd pulled Cooper into the house and toward Alpha Carter's office. He knocked, waited until the alpha told him to open, and pushed Cooper through before following him into the room.

"What's going on?" Alpha Carter asked.

He was sitting behind his desk, and Cooper wondered if he was actually working or if he was watching porn. Since he'd caught the alpha masturbating in his office more than once, he wouldn't be surprised at either of those options. He looked dressed, though, so he'd probably been working. Cooper wasn't sure which interruption was worse in the alpha's eyes, but either way, he knew a beating was coming his way. Hopefully, Alpha Carter wouldn't break anything this time.

"I found him in the garden," Beta Boyd said. Cooper glared at him.

"In the garden, huh? What were you doing out there, Cooper?"

Cooper sighed. Not answering would only make things worse. "I was checking the flowers."

"The flowers?"

"Yes. I like being in the garden and tending to them."

"Yet you're forbidden from leaving the house. How did you get out?"

There was no way Cooper was telling them about it. His bedroom window was supposed to be locked, and it had been once. But Cooper had managed to break the lock, even though looking at it, you couldn't tell. "The back door. There was no one in the kitchen, and I snuck out. I just wanted to see the flowers."

Alpha Carter rose from his chair, and Cooper steeled himself. He saw the backhand coming, and even though he was expecting it, it didn't help him stay upright. He stumbled back and knocked against Beta Boyd. The man growled and pushed Cooper forward.

Cooper never knew if it was better to face the beatings on

his feet or on the floor. He almost always started on his feet, but would his not falling make the alpha even angrier? The man liked being bowed to, having the visual that he was the better, more powerful man.

Cooper slid to his knees, ignoring the throbbing in his cheek.

The second hit made his head snap back. At least it was on the other cheek, although considering how much it hurt, maybe it wasn't a good thing. Cooper didn't know. He just wanted this to be over so he could go lick his wounds in his bedroom.

He was grateful and relieved when Alpha Carter ordered Beta Boyd to take him to his room and lock him in. It meant he wouldn't get lunch, and probably not even dinner, but he'd be able to tend to his wounds, curl in his bed, and rest.

This nightmare would be there when he woke up tomorrow morning, and the day after that, until he finally found the courage to leave. Every punch, every slap, was a step toward that decision. Cooper was going to have to make it before things got too bad, though. He wasn't sure why, but Alpha Carter was becoming more violent, especially with him.

If he didn't leave, he was probably going to die under the alpha's hands, and no one would care. How sad was that?

CHAPTER TWO

"I wish the entire team were here," Michael grumbled as he, Pryderi, and Justin met in the living room in the enforcers' wing.

"Still bitchy? I thought you'd be happy that you're finally allowed to get back to work," Pryderi said. He was adjusting his uniform, but Michael saw the smile on his lips.

"Oh, I *am* happy about it. It's better than being forced to veg on the couch. I miss the rest of the team, though. Well, some of them. Sasha can keep Hunter, for all I care."

Justin snorted, but he didn't say anything. Michael grinned at him. He wanted Justin to feel like he belonged with their team, like he was part of their small family — because he did, and he was.

Pryderi bumped his fist against Michael's shoulder. "You'd be lost without him."

"Me? I don't think so." But they both knew it was bullshit. Hunter was Michael's best friend, and he lived with the fear that Hunter might decide to ask for a transfer to Gillham, or that he'd quit the enforcers. Michael would never say anything about it, and he couldn't deny it would be easy enough to visit Hunter if he did move to Gillham, but it wouldn't be the same. Right now, he and the team spent days, sometimes weeks, together, eating and joking around, working and protecting each other. They wouldn't have that anymore if Hunter left, and Michael hated the thought. He'd be supportive if that was what Hunter decided to do, of course, but that didn't mean he'd be happy about it.

"Ready?" Pryderi asked.

Michael nodded. "Justin?"

"Where are we going?"

"A town called Green Hill, or rather, a pride that lives close to it. The council hasn't been able to make contact with them in the past few years, and they're worried about the conditions the pride members are living in."

"Why?"

"Well, from what I was able to find out, the alpha was deemed an asshole by several people who left the pride. That's one of the reasons the council is sending us there."

"What can we expect to find?"

Michael scratched his jaw. "There's no real way to know, unfortunately, but I managed to find an enforcer who used to be part of the pride, and I gave him a call last night. He said that the alpha was an asshole and a controlling one at that. I wouldn't be surprised if the guy has gotten worse over the years and is keeping his pride members prisoners. That means he probably has to resort to violence." Michael doubted anyone would stick around without that kind of *incentive*.

"How do we deal with it?"

"Dominic and Emerson want us to reach out and assess the situation. We can put a foot in the door, but not barge in. We need enough information to give ourselves an idea of what's going on and report. Emerson and the council will then decide what to do, which might include sending us back with the rest of the team. Emerson said he'd texted all of them to make them aware of the fact that I was ready to get back to work and that they needed to wrap things up. You didn't get it?"

Justin shrugged. "Maybe. I don't check my phone that often."

"All right. Let's head out."

They walked to the room reserved for shimmering in and out of the wing. The infirmary was right next to it, and Michael stuck his tongue out at Jared as he passed by the open door. Jared laughed, and the sound followed Michael to the shimmering room. He smiled. He knew Jared just wanted the best for everyone, but especially for the Whitedell pride members. There were a lot of them, but they were all family, and they took care of each other.

"You have the address?" Michael asked Pryderi.

Pryderi nodded. He'd have checked the pictures they had of the area to give himself an idea of what he had to think of when he shimmered. Sometimes, things like the topography had changed from when the pictures had been taken, but even then, Pryderi was always able to get them close enough. He'd honed his ability to shimmer over the years, and he was great at it, better than most of the Nix Michael had shimmered with.

Michael and Justin took Pryderi's offered hands. Michael didn't close his eyes like he used to in the beginning. He was used to shimmering. He'd done it hundreds of times, if not more, and trips with Pryderi were always smooth.

They arrived in front of a closed gate. Michael peered around, noticing the high fence that no doubt ran around the entire perimeter of pride territory.

"Cameras," Justin grunted.

Michael nodded and looked up. There was a camera pointed at the gate so the people inside the big house he could see from where he was would know who was there. He noticed another one, still pointed at the road that led through the gate. There didn't seem to be others, but Michael wouldn't have been surprised if they were there, hidden.

"Who's ringing the bell?" Pryderi asked.

Michael shrugged. "I'll do it." He had a pretty good idea what to expect from the people inside the house, and he wasn't disappointed.

He pressed the button and waited. The intercom crackled, and a brusque voice asked, "Who is it?"

"Hello, my name is Michael, and I'm an enforcer. I've been sent by the council to check on this pride."

"We don't want you here."

Yep. No surprise there. "I understand that, and I'll leave as soon as I can talk to—" There was a clang, and Michael blinked. "Did they hang up on me?" he asked Pryderi.

"I'm pretty sure they did."

Michael pressed the button again, but he wasn't surprised he didn't get an answer. "They're not going to open."

"No shit, Sherlock," Justin muttered.

Michael glared at him. "You're not helping. Why are you here again, if you're not helping?"

Justin flexed his arms. "I'm the muscle."

Michael rolled his eyes. Now wasn't the moment to play around, but he was glad for it, and for Justin's presence.

"What do we do?" Pryderi asked.

"Well, Emerson said we needed to at least check in with someone. Can you shimmer us to the front door?"

"Sure, unless they have a blocker."

"What do you think?"

"Can't know until I try." He held his hands out. Michael and Justin took them, and off they were.

"You'd think they'd have thought about buying blockers," Justin murmured when they appeared in front of the door.

"Especially with a Nix tribe living close by," Michael agreed. He raised his hand and knocked on the door.

He wasn't shocked when it opened and he was met with a gun.

He raised his hands. "There's no need to use that. I'm just here to ask a few questions," he said, hoping to soothe the man glaring at him.

"I told you, we don't want to talk to you or any of your kind."

Michael could see part of the entrance around the guy. It was well-cared for, with dark wood furniture and floor, light blue walls, and even paintings on the walls. If there was something odd going on, it wasn't a neglected household. That didn't mean the pride members weren't abused and maltreated. "I understand that, but unfortunately, you have to. We're with the council, and —"

The guy waved the gun. "I don't care who you're with. You need to leave before I shoot your ass."

Michael exchanged a glance with Justin. They wouldn't barge into the house, and Michael didn't want to. They *were* going to get shot if they tried. But this kind of behavior was indicative that there *was* a problem, and Michael would bring it up to Emerson. They'd have to come back with the rest of the team.

Then he smelled it.

He didn't know what it was, not for the first few seconds. As the scent filled his nose — flowers and trees, fresh cut grass — it hit him.

His mate was somewhere in the house.

Michael leaned forward to try to understand if it was the man with the gun, but no, it wasn't. The man frowned and cocked the gun, and someone — Justin — grabbed the back of Michael's shirt and pulled him back.

"We're leaving," he growled.

And before he knew it, Michael was shimmered away.

****

Cooper knew something was happening. He had no idea what, and he had no way to find out, not from the kitchen.

He looked around. He was alone right now, peeling about a thousand carrots for dinner. Everyone had disappeared when he'd started because they didn't want to risk being roped into helping. Cooper would have followed them right out if he could have gotten out of it.

Maybe he could go see what was happening. He'd have to be fast and sneak back to the kitchen, but he could do it. He'd gotten good at sneaking around over the years.

He put down his knife and the carrot he'd been working on, then inched toward the open kitchen door. Voices were coming from the entrance. Cooper recognized Beta Boyd's, then the unmistakable sound of the gun being cocked. He had no idea who the people at the door were, though.

They didn't often have visitors. The pride was isolated, and Cooper didn't think anyone had come to their door in at least a decade, if not more. People knew better than to do so, because they'd be met by a gun and angry tiger shifters.

So who else was there? Cooper didn't recognize the voice. He tiptoed along the hallway until he could hear better. He couldn't see the front door because he didn't want to risk being noticed, but it was good enough.

And it allowed him to smell the man at the door. He knew what that scent meant as soon as it hit his nose. He'd yearned for it for a long time, had heard stories about it. Of course, almost no one in the pride was bonded, because Alpha Carter wouldn't let them leave the house to find their mate. Cooper suspected that even if one of them did somehow find their other half, Alpha Carter wouldn't care. He hadn't when his nephew's wife had met hers, and the council had had to intervene. They'd been alerted by the Nix tribe, though.

No one would tell them about Cooper, even though there

were laws that forbid anyone to keep mates separated.

He had to get to the front door. He had to get to his mate. He wouldn't get a second chance. He was sure of that.

He moved forward, ready to push past Beta Boyd even if he had to throw the man to the floor.

He never got there. An arm wrapped around his waist and pulled him back while a hand clamped against his mouth.

Cooper tried to scream, but the hand muffled the sound, and he heard the front door slam shut before he could try again. That didn't mean he stopped fighting, though.

He kicked back and wiggled, trying to get away, and when that didn't work, he bit the hand on his mouth. The man who'd grabbed him swore and Cooper realized his mistake. *Alpha Carter* had been holding him back. Cooper had bitten him, and from the taste in his mouth, had drawn blood.

This wasn't going to end well, and if Cooper didn't calm down, it would be worse. Right now, Alpha Carter didn't know that the man who'd knocked on their front door was Cooper's mate, so he wouldn't do anything to try to stop Cooper from leaving because he didn't *know* Cooper wanted to leave.

He stopped fighting.

Alpha Carter pushed him against the wall, and Cooper bit his lower lip so he wouldn't cry out in pain. His cheek was pressed against the rough surface of the wall, and Alpha Carter was pinning him there, his hand around the back of Cooper's neck.

"What the fuck is going on here?" Alpha Carter boomed.

Cooper's face was turned the other way, so he didn't see Beta Boyd come closer, but he heard him. "The council sent someone."

"The council?"

"Yes. Enforcers. Three of them, all male. They wanted to come in and to talk to you."

"Who the fuck let them through the gate?"

"No one. They shimmered in." There was a pause. "They wouldn't have been able to if we'd bought those blockers."

"Don't you think I know that? But unless you pay for them, I don't have the money. Actually, that's probably not a bad idea."

Cooper hadn't known the pride had money problems, but he wasn't surprised. Alpha Carter liked to think he was a good alpha, but he was an incompetent asshole who wouldn't have gotten the job if his father hadn't been the alpha before him.

"Alpha—"

"You'll go buy them tomorrow. How many did that guy say we needed to cover the entire territory?"

"Three, but—"

"You'll go tomorrow." Alpha Carter finally released Cooper.

Cooper slid to the floor, but Alpha Carter grabbed his hair and pulled him up. Cooper cried out, then bit his lower lip so hard he broke the skin because he didn't want to give Alpha Carter the satisfaction of hearing him in pain. His mouth tasted of blood, and he knew it would continue to do so, but he could get through it. He always did.

Alpha Carter dragged him upstairs. Cooper did his best to keep up because the alpha was still pulling on his hair. He stumbled up the stairs, and Alpha Carter threw him into the hallway in the direction of his bedroom. "Get the fuck to your room," he snarled.

Cooper scrambled toward his door. He got a kick to the legs as he did so, but it could have been so much worse. It *should* have been worse.

The door slammed behind him. He heard the key in the

lock and breathed better. He was locked inside, and while that wasn't great, it was better than to be in Alpha Carter's hands, especially now.

Alpha Carter slammed his fist against the door. "You're lucky I need to go back downstairs and see what kind of a mess Boyd made. But I'll be back, Cooper, and you'll be punished." There was another slam, then the sound of footsteps moving away.

Cooper leaned the back of his head against the wall and closed his eyes. He probably had an hour, maybe a little more, before Alpha Carter was done talking to and yelling at Beta Boyd. They'd need some time to find out what had happened and why the council was sending people to their house.

Cooper had to get out of there.

Ideally, he could pack some of the things he'd accumulated and hidden over the years. He could leave everything behind if he had to, but he'd rather not. He knew that if he went, he'd never come back.

And that was okay. Cooper didn't have anything keeping him there. He loved his parents, but he hated them at the same time because they'd never done anything to help him. They'd bowed to Alpha Carter, and they would continue to do so.

Cooper would never be allowed to leave the pride, not even if he told Alpha Carter his mate was one of the men outside. Alpha Carter would probably chain him to the wall if he found out. Then he'd make sure no one ever found out about it, and Cooper didn't have a way to find out if his mate had smelled him or not. As far as he knew, his mate had no clue he was there and that they were mates, and he'd never come back. Why would he?

So Cooper had to get out on his own. He had a way, although he'd never been able to get outside the fence. He'd have to be fast, do it while Alpha Carter was busy with Beta Boyd.

The sound of the key in the lock startled Cooper. Alpha Carter couldn't already be done. *Right?*

But he was. His eyes sparkled with the promise of pain as he closed the door behind himself. "Why did you run toward the front door earlier?" he asked.

Cooper licked his lips. He couldn't answer that, not truthfully. "I wanted them to take me away."

That earned him the first slap. Some days, he wondered if his bruises were ever going to heal fully.

"So you think you're better than the pride," Alpha Carter said.

"No. Just better than you." If Cooper was going to leave, then he might as well say what was on his mind before he did. Of course, Alpha Carter might beat him so hard that he wouldn't be able to go now, but that was okay. He'd made his decision, and he wasn't changing his mind.

He'd get out of this house, one way or another, sooner or later.

****

"Did you hear that?" Michael asked. He looked around, wondering where Pryderi had shimmered them. He'd hoped it would be outside the gate, but of course, Pryderi had taken them home.

"Hear what?" Justin asked.

"Someone cried out just as we were leaving. We have to go back."

Pryderi patted Michael's shoulder. "We will, but it's obvious the three of us won't be enough. I'm not exactly looking forward to being shot."

"Pryderi, they don't have blockers. That means you can

shimmer right in and go *around* the gun."

Pryderi frowned. "Yeah, but I'm also not allowed to do that. You know it."

Michael raked a hand through his hair. He couldn't be sure that the person who'd cried out had been his mate, but what were the odds? He'd smelled him, and someone had been trying to get to him. It *had* to have been his mate. "You don't understand." He paced the length of the shimmering room, trying to find a way to convince Pryderi to go.

"You're right, we don't understand," Pryderi admitted. "Why don't you explain what the problem is?"

"What happened?" Emerson said, striding in.

Michael huffed. He didn't need to be given more red tape. He needed to go back, and to go back *now*. Who knew what was happening at that house right now? What was being done to his mate? Because there was no way Michael could believe the people living there were happy, not when visitors were greeted with guns.

Michael groaned when he noticed a few team members drifting in behind Emerson. He did *not* want to have to make a public announcement, not about this. Although maybe that wasn't a bad idea, now that he thought about it. His friends would want to go back to help his mate as much as he did.

"We have to go back," he told Emerson.

Emerson frowned. "Can you tell me what happened before you decide to barge into that pride's house in a way you shouldn't, since you work for the council?"

Michael breathed in and out, trying to calm himself. "We went there and buzzed the intercom. They told us to fuck off. So we shimmered right to the front door and knocked, and they opened it holding a gun. They don't want to talk to us. They don't want to let us in. And my mate lives there."

There was no reason for Michael to hide that bit of info. It would probably make things worse if he did.

He swallowed. "And just as Pryderi was shimmering us back, I heard someone cry out. I *know* it's him. I know he was trying to get to me, and that he was stopped. We need to go back."

Emerson grabbed Michael's arm to stop him. "Breathe, Michael. We're going to take care of this. I know you're worried about your mate, but we can't rush back, not when we don't know what's going on. You said there were guns?"

Michael was glad when Pryderi took over. "One of them, at least. The guy who opened the door seemed intent on using it, too."

"We need to sit down and plan this. I don't want anyone to be hurt, and I don't want people to have a reason to blame the enforcers if something goes wrong."

Michael had to force himself to listen. He knew Emerson was right, but he was panicking. He couldn't stop thinking about what was happening to his mate. He'd been trying to get to Michael, but they hadn't allowed him to. Did that mean they were punishing him right now? Beating him? Or worse?

"Stop it," Justin huffed.

Michael blinked up at him. "What?"

"You're thinking the worst."

"What would you think if you were in my position?"

Justin wrinkled his nose. "I get it, but you can't focus on that. Think about your mate and the fact that by the end of the day, he'll be with you here, safe."

Because that wasn't terrifying. "Right." Justin *was* right. Michael would go crazy if he thought about what was happening in that house right now. He wasn't sure of anything except that his mate was in there, and he needed to focus on getting him out.

"I texted the rest of your team. They'll meet us in the conference room," Emerson said.

Michael followed him and the others outside. He was on autopilot, because no matter what Justin had said, he couldn't stop thinking about his mate. He tried to avoid bad thoughts, though. They'd only make this harder.

They had to wait until the entire team was around the table to start, and it felt like an eternity. Michael bounced his knees, ignoring the glare that earned him, and tried to focus on the future. His mate *was* going to be here by the end of the day. What would they do? Michael wasn't sure that offering to share his bedroom was a good idea since they didn't know each other yet, but was there an empty guest room nearby? And what if Michael's mate didn't want to stay with the pride, or if he didn't want Michael?

Pryderi squeezed Michael's shoulder, and Michael was grateful for the interruption. "Stop obsessing over this," he murmured.

"I can't." Not even if he tried, he suspected.

"I know it's hard, but it's useless to think about what's going to happen after we get him back to Gillham."

"I know. I just want to be ready in case he'd rather stay with the Green Hill pride."

Pryderi grimaced. "I don't see why he'd want that, but if he does, we'll find a way to help, okay?"

Michael hoped he was right.

By the time he'd thought about all the questions he could think about and then some, the entire team had arrived. Hunter looked like he wanted to ask Michael what was happening, but Emerson cleared his throat before he could, and Michael was glad for that. He was going to have to explain to everyone anyway, and the sooner they were done, the sooner they'd be able to go back to Green Hill.

"Thank you for coming in," Emerson said. "Michael? You should explain what happened."

Michael groaned. He hated being the center of attention,

even when it came to his team. Still, he needed to do this. "I went with Justin and Pryderi to visit the Green Hill pride this morning. The council wanted us to assess them, their alpha, and the way he treats his people since the pride hasn't been communicating with the council and has been ignoring e-mails and phone calls. They wouldn't let us in, and when we got to the front door, they greeted us with a gun. Now, I realize that might only mean that they're wary of strangers, even though we identified ourselves as council enforcers, but I think we should investigate this. If they aren't doing anything wrong, they shouldn't have a problem with us talking to the pride members. Even if they don't want us inside their house, we could talk to them in the garden." Michael swallowed. "Also, while we were there, I smelled my mate."

He'd half expected congratulations and whatnot, but everyone was focused on what he was saying, and that was a good thing. He didn't care about congratulations, not when he didn't have his mate with him, and he didn't even know if his mate was okay.

"I didn't see him, just smelled him, and I heard someone cry out just as Pryderi shimmered us out."

"I shimmered us because the guy looked like he wouldn't have minded shooting us," Pryderi said.

"I know."

Sarah raised her hand. "So you don't know what's happening in that house."

"No."

"But you think we should investigate. You suspect the pride members aren't treated well."

"Yes."

She leaned back in her chair. "The way I see it, you're probably right, but I'd suggest a softer approach."

"What do you mean?"

"Well, you said you smelled your mate in there, right? Are you sure about that?"

"Yes." Michael had never been surer of anything.

"Then you have a right at the very least to see him. I'd suggest having the entire team there as a back-up, but you should ask to see the alpha because your mate lives there and because you have a right to talk to him. If the alpha refuses, he's in the wrong, and we can act. But this will keep us on the side of the law."

No matter how much Michael wanted to charge into the house and save his mate, he knew Sarah was right.

****

Cooper's entire body hurt. He didn't think anything was broken, and he wasn't sure how that had happened. Alpha Carter hadn't gone easy on him. He never did, of course, but this time, it felt like he'd been particularly dedicated to his task, or at least that was what it had felt like on the other side of his fists and kicks.

Cooper rolled over and groaned. No one would come help him, so he had to get to his feet and start moving.

He slowly moved his arms and legs, but apart from the pain from the normal ache from the hits, he was okay. He managed to push himself into a sitting position and gently touched his face. It hurt—of course it did—and he could feel blood oozing from his lips and a cut above his eye.

Once he was sure he wouldn't faint or anything, he got to his feet. He felt like an eighty-year-old man, and he had to lean against the wall to keep the room still because his head spun.

Shit. This was bad. Not as bad as some of the other beatings Cooper had gotten, but if he wanted to be able to leave the pride tonight, he needed to be able to walk and slide down the trellis. That meant taking painkillers and tending to his wounds as well as he could.

He shuffled to his nightstand and dropped onto the bed. He had to reach under the nightstand to grab the box that contained the painkillers and the stuff he needed for his wounds. His mother had snuck the box to him a few years ago, and she refilled it when he needed it. Cooper wasn't sure what that meant, and he didn't want to think about it right now because nothing could stop him from getting out. He might want to stick around for his mom if he let himself think about the times she'd tried to help him, and he couldn't do that. He couldn't allow anything to keep him here because sooner or later, he wouldn't be able to leave anymore, not if Alpha Carter continued to beat him the way he'd just done.

There was a small mirror in the box, and Cooper grimaced when he saw his reflection. His lower lip was split, and the cut above his eye was still bleeding. Most of his face was black and blue, with some yellow where the oldest bruises were fading. Some blood had trickled down his chin and to his neck, and he wiped it off with the disinfectant wipes his mom had put in the box.

Once he was done with his face, he took his clothes off. Most of his body was in the same state as his face, with bruises covering most of his skin. There was thankfully little blood — Alpha Carter had perfected his style of beating because he didn't like the pride members to be out of business for long. He needed them to do housework and cater to him after all.

Cooper had some cuts on his hands and arms from when he'd shielded his face with them, but they were easily dealt with. He'd ache and be sore for a while, but after carefully moving and putting away the box, he thought he could make it.

The problem was, what would he do once he was out of the house? He'd have to find a way to climb the fence, and he wasn't sure he could, not in the state he was in. And what if he did manage but couldn't get away fast enough? Even if he shifted, Alpha Carter and the others had cars. They'd come after him, and with his entire body hurting, he wasn't sure he'd manage to make it.

Cooper had to try, though. He wasn't sure how he'd do it, but he wanted to find his mate, and he couldn't do that if he cowered in his bedroom. He didn't want to wait for his mate or anyone else to come save him. He wanted to save himself, even if it meant Alpha Carter caught him and killed him. That would be better than living the way he had for his entire life, but especially for the past decade or so. He'd had enough of being beaten, of having to keep quiet because he'd get hurt if he talked.

He wanted out, dammit.

He was angry, so he got up and banged on his bedroom door. "Open the door!" he yelled even though he knew it wasn't going to help. Hell, the most probable outcome of this would be to bring Alpha Carter back to his room, but he'd had enough. If Alpha Carter came back, he'd shift and attack the asshole, even if it killed him. He didn't care anymore.

Except he did.

Cooper lowered his arms. Okay, that wasn't the smartest idea. He didn't want to die, for fuck's sake. He wanted to live, to free himself and to find his mate. He wanted to fall in love with the guy and spend the rest of his life with him, happy and doing whatever the fuck he wanted with his life.

He pushed away from the door. He needed to pack. He didn't have a lot of personal stuff, but he'd accumulated some over the years, and there was no way he'd leave it behind.

Someone pounded on the door, making him jump. His heart raced, and he held his breath.

"Shut the fuck up, Cooper!" Beta Boyd said with a growl.

He wasn't as dangerous as Alpha Carter. He didn't beat people. He just obeyed orders, and while that made him an asshole and a coward, Cooper was pretty sure he wouldn't come in, not even if Cooper cursed him. "Fuck you!" he yelled back, and it felt *so* good.

Cooper had kept his mouth shut and his head down for so long. He'd lost hope he'd ever leave this place. But now he knew he would, one way or another, and he wasn't going to leave quietly.

"What the fuck did you say?"

Cooper hit the door. "I said, fuck you! You're an asshole. Alpha Carter is an asshole. And you're both going to pay for this."

"Just shut up, Cooper."

"One of them is my mate, you know? And I'm sure he knows it and that he's going to come back for me. You're going to pay for keeping us apart. It's against the law."

Silence met Cooper's words, and he wondered if he'd freaked Beta Boyd out or if he was trying to think about a creative way to get him to shut up.

"You're lying," Beta Boyd finally said, but Cooper could hear the doubt in his voice.

"You can try convincing yourself of that. But wouldn't it be better for you and the rest of the pride to let me go? You might be able to keep the enforcers happy if you do."

"Because you wouldn't tell them about everything that happens around here?"

"I promise I won't. I don't care about anyone here. I don't care what happens to them. I just want to be free."

"Just—shut up, Cooper. You don't want Alpha Carter to come around again, do you?"

Cooper wanted to rage against the coward, but he needed to start moving, to pack and then rest. He wasn't sure why his mate had come to the house, but if he was an enforcer, the way he'd been sent away might mean he was going to come back. Cooper had no way to know if he'd do that today or tomorrow, but in either case, he wanted to be ready. If he heard something, anything weird, he'd get out of the house and pray someone was there and could save him.

He hated the thought of not being able to save himself, but he'd take what he got. At this point, he didn't care if it made him weak in the eyes of other people. As long as he was out of here, out of hell, he'd be fine, whatever people thought about him.

He strode to the closet—or he moved as fast as he could, anyway. He was limping slightly, and he hoped it wouldn't hinder him when he climbed off the roof and down the trellis tomorrow. He took an old bag he'd saved from the trash a few years ago and opened it, dropping it onto the bed. Then he looked around.

The few books he loved went in there. They were old and falling to pieces, but he wasn't allowed to buy other books, and he cared for them. They'd been the companions of long and lonely painful nights, and he wasn't going to leave them behind.

He added some clothes, his hairbrush, a dried flower he'd kept from the garden, his toothbrush. When he looked at the little pile, it was painfully small and pathetic, and he promised himself that once he was out, he'd buy all the stuff he'd wanted over the years.

He deserved them. He deserved *everything*.

CHAPTER THREE

Michael had wanted to go back right away, but Sarah and Emerson had agreed it was best to wait. He hated that, but he wasn't the one in charge, and no matter how many times he'd asked Nysys, the Nix had refused to shimmer him back to Green Hill. He'd said something about having enough of playing hero, and Michael knew it had to do with the time he and Sasha had shimmered to the jungle to save him and Hunter.

At least it was early in the morning, so early that the sky outside was still dark.

"All right, people. Gather around," Sarah said.

Michael rolled his eyes. "We've already been through this."

Sarah glared. "And we'll go through it again because we're not barging in there halfcocked to get ourselves killed. Do I have to remind you that those guys have at least one gun and are tiger shifters? I'd rather not have anyone dead or hurt by the end of the day, and especially not you, so if you can't behave the way you were trained to, I'm going to order you to stay here."

Michael raised his hands. "I'll shut up, and I'll be careful."

Sarah sighed. "I know. And I know you need to get your mate. I understand that. We're doing everything we can to help, but we're council enforcers. That means we have to do things the right way."

"I know."

"Good." She went back over the plan, making sure every

team member knew what they were going to do.

Michael wanted to kiss Pryderi when he finally shimmered them in front of the gate. Everyone was tense and ready to defend themselves, but they were alone. The sun was peeking up at the horizon, and from where they were, Michael could see lights on in the house. Someone was awake, and they needed to be careful.

"Shouldn't we have waited until a decent hour?" Hunter asked.

"What, you also wanted to give them a call to tell them we were coming maybe?"

"Well, no, but Sarah said she wanted to do this the right way, with you, knocking on the door and demanding to see your mate. I mean, I'd be pissed if someone knocked on my door at six in the morning."

"It's not six."

"Feels like it."

Michael rolled his eyes and turned toward Pryderi. "You think they had the time to get blockers?"

"There's only one way to find out."

Sarah had decided to send Michael, Pryderi, and Justin again since the man who'd opened already knew them. Michael wasn't sure that would change anything, but she was the boss, and as long as they managed to get his mate out of the house, he didn't care who went with him.

He and Justin took Pryderi's hands, and Pryderi shimmered them to the front door. "No blockers."

"Yet, so we better hurry up," Justin said. He raised his hand and knocked on the door.

Everything was silent for a while, then Michael heard footsteps. He tensed, knowing they were about to see the gun again.

"Who the fuck is this?" a voice growled from behind the

door.

Michael cleared his throat. "I'm Michael. I came around yesterday. I'm a council enforcer."

"I told you to fuck off."

"I know, but, sir, my mate lives in this house, and as you know, there are laws in place that say you can't keep us apart."

There was a pause. "Wait there."

Michael wasn't going anywhere.

"Do you think they're going to be nicer this time around?" Pryderi asked.

Justin snorted. "Yeah, right."

That was pretty much what Michael was thinking, so he didn't add anything. There was no way this was going to end well, but as long as he had his mate, he was okay with whatever outcome.

The footsteps came back, this time accompanied by angrier ones. The door swung open, and Michael steeled himself.

The man in front of them was bare-chested and glaring. "What the fuck do you want?" he snapped.

Michael had to stop himself from telling the guy to fuck off. Sarah was right—he *was* too close to this. That wasn't going to make him stop, though. "I came by yesterday. The council wants me and my team to check in on you and your pride members."

"Everyone's fine."

"I'm sure they are, Alpha Carter." The guy hadn't introduced himself, but Michael thought it was pretty evident that he was the alpha.

"Then you can leave."

"Not yet. We haven't checked in on your pride members, and more importantly, I smelled my mate yesterday, when I came."

"Your mate. Who would that be?"

"I don't know. I wasn't allowed to come in."

"And you still aren't. You need to leave."

"I understand you don't want me here, but you can't forbid me to talk to my mate. You'd be arrested."

"For fuck's sake. Everyone in the house is either too young, married, or bonded. There's nothing for you here."

Michael's heart broke a little at the thought of his mate in a relationship, married, but he pushed the pain away. He'd seen this situation more than once. It was never easy, but that didn't mean it didn't work. "Well, I'm sure that if we talk—"

"I'm not going to let you bug the shit out of my people, and I don't care what you claim about that mate shit. I told you, there's no one available for you here, and if you don't leave, I'll make you." He extended his arm, and the man from yesterday, who'd been standing close by, handed him a gun.

This wasn't going well. Michael wanted to try one last time, though. "Alpha Carter, I'm sure you realize that your refusal to let me see my mate means the council can have you arrested."

The alpha aimed the gun toward Michael. "Do I look like I care about your fucking council? Leave, and don't come back, because you *will* be shot if you do."

Michael didn't doubt that. He wanted to push his way in, to insist, to go find his mate, but instead, he held his hand out to Pryderi. "We'll be back with reinforcements, Alpha Carter. I'm sorry things had to go that way."

Michael was glad Pryderi shimmered them away, because he was pretty sure the alpha would have shot him otherwise.

They reappeared outside the gate, and Sarah arched a brow in question. Michael shook his head. He hadn't expected to be able to get to his mate this way. After the way things had gone yesterday, he'd known things would be hard. He just hoped his mate was okay and that he wouldn't get hurt for something he had no control over.

Sarah sighed. "All right. We'll stay around for a bit, check if anyone is leaving the house to go to work. I'd rather not have to face the entire pride since we don't know how many members there are. Michael, did you get anything at all from whoever you talked to?"

"Just the impression that Alpha Carter doesn't like the council and doesn't care that he can be arrested for keeping my mate away from me."

"That's not helpful. Okay, people, you know what happens next. We go in, arrest the alpha and the beta if he has anything to do with this, and talk to the pride members. Be careful and don't let your guard down with anyone. We have no way of knowing if they're kept here against their will or if they want to stay, so don't underestimate anyone. Michael, your main job is to find your mate. Once you do, talk to him. We don't know how he'll take this, but hopefully, he can shed some light over what's happening here."

Finding his mate was going to be easier said than done. Michael would recognize him by smell, and he was the only one who could do that, but with so many people living in the house, his mate's scent was bound to be buried, especially if he was being kept away. Michael didn't want to think that maybe he *wanted* to stay away because he wanted nothing to do with Michael.

He had to believe they could at least talk, that he'd have a chance at this kind of happiness. He was ready for it after years of watching his brother and his friends, and he was going to do everything in his power to make sure he at least got a shot at it.

****

They were back. Cooper would have heard it even if Alpha Carter hadn't been yelling at Beta Boyd for opening the door to them.

Cooper's mate was back.

Or at least he hoped so. He couldn't hear what Alpha Carter was saying apart from a few words here and there, so he had no way to know if his mate was one of the enforcers today. Besides, it wasn't like he knew what the guy looked like. No, he only knew his scent and that he was an enforcer — and he hoped he was still out there.

He rushed to the window and peeked outside. His bedroom looked out on the gate and the front yard, and with the sun rising, he could see a group of people outside the gate, watching the house. The enforcers hadn't left — yet — so this was the right moment. Cooper *had* to take advantage of this, because he doubted he'd get another chance. Alpha Carter would be focused on the enforcers and the reasons they weren't leaving, and maybe, if Cooper was lucky, he could run to the gate and have them help him around it before anyone noticed he was gone.

He looked at his bedroom door, listened for a moment, then rushed around the room, pushing pillows under his blanket in what he hoped looked like a sleeping person and grabbing his backpack. He slowly pushed the window open, careful not to make noise and thankful he'd thought of keeping it well-oiled.

He was about to swing one leg outside when the key turned in the lock. He froze, knowing he probably looked like a deer in headlights. He stayed that way only a few seconds before he scrambled to try to close the window, but it was too late.

His mom stepped in. She quickly closed the door, then her gaze went to the bed, and finally, to Cooper. Her eyes widened. There was no way she didn't understand what was going on, not when Cooper was next to the open window with his bag in his hand. "Cooper?"

Cooper swallowed. What could he say to have her let him go without kicking up a fuss? "Mom."

Her expression softened. "What's going on?"

Cooper waved toward the window. "Some council enforcers are here."

"I know that. *Why* are they here?"

"I have no idea. One of them is my mate, though, so maybe he smelled me yesterday, and he's come back for me." Cooper prayed that was the case, but if it wasn't, maybe he could ask these enforcers if they knew who his mate was. Of course, he'd have to get to them before anyone realized what he was doing, and he doubted that would be possible, not if his mother tried to stop him. "I need to go to him, Mom."

"But . . . you can't leave the pride. You can't leave me."

Cooper resisted the urge to roll his eyes. *Now* she was interested in him? "I have to leave. I can't stand another beating." He waved at his face. "You see this. He's going to kill me eventually, and even if he doesn't, I don't deserve to live this way. No one does."

Cooper's body still ached, but he would make it. He had to. He could rest and heal once he was out of this hell. Until then, he'd push through the pain.

Her shoulders sagged. "I know you don't. I hate that you have to go through this."

Cooper snorted. "Yeah? You've never told me that. You've never tried to stop Alpha Carter. You've never helped me tend to my wounds."

"Because I couldn't. The few times I tried, he was even harder on you, to teach me not to defy him."

Cooper hadn't known that. He wasn't surprised at how much of an asshole Alpha Carter was, but he wasn't sure it healed all the pain and suffering his mother's behavior had created. He understood where she came from now, and maybe if he had a child, he'd behave the same way, but understanding his mom didn't mean he was going to stay. "He's going to kill me if I stay."

She wrung her fingers. "What's going to happen to you? What will you do?"

"I'm not sure. I'll ask those enforcers to get me out. I don't know if what Alpha Carter has done to me over the years will be enough for them to be able to prosecute him and put his ass in jail, but I hope it is, and I'll testify against him. He doesn't deserve to be an alpha."

Cooper had never really thought about what his options would be if he managed to leave the pride, but maybe he could help the others. He didn't have friends, just his parents, but he didn't think he could ignore what was going on here without hating himself. Once he managed to do something about it, he'd be able to live his life without regrets or without wondering if Alpha Carter had started regularly beating someone else. The fact that he had a young wife and a newborn made Cooper afraid he'd turn to them, and that wasn't something he wanted to allow, not if he could somehow stop it.

"Let me go, Mom. Please." He hoped he could convince her to keep her mouth shut until he was on the other side of the gate, but he'd take anything right now. "No one knows you came in here and found me. Hell, you're not *allowed* to be here, so you could go back to your room and act like you don't know anything."

"Alpha Carter is going to be angry."

"I know." And he hated the thought, because it meant Alpha Carter would retaliate on someone, but he couldn't think of the others right now. He couldn't, even though his first instinct was to do just that. For once, he had to think of himself in a way no one ever had, not even his mother, not even him. "And I'm sorry. But I don't want to die. I want to find my mate and have a happy life with him. I'll do what I can to make sure Alpha Carter pays for what he's done and what he's still doing, but I need to think of myself, Mom." The way she should have.

Because Cooper couldn't believe she'd never had an opportunity to help him escape. Even if Alpha Carter had threatened her to hurt him more, she didn't spend half her days locked in her room. She could have found a way to help Cooper to run, and maybe, she could have run with him. It was too late for that, though.

Cooper's mom looked back at the door. "Go. I'll lock it again and go downstairs to try to distract Alpha Carter. I don't know if it's going to be possible, not with your friends out there, but I'll do my best. You don't have much time, though."

Cooper nodded. He wasn't sure he'd ever see her again, and he surprised both of them when he wrapped his arms around her and squeezed. "Thank you."

She patted his back. "I know I haven't been the best mother, but I still love you, and if you can be safe and happy, then you have to give it a try. Go, Cooper. Live your life."

Cooper was going to do just that. He waited until his mom was out of the room and he heard the key turn in the lock again. Then he rushed back to the window and scrambled out of it. He had to be careful not to fall off the roof, especially when he had to lower himself onto the trellis. His arms and legs hurt, the bruises pulling with every movement he made.

Once he was on the ground, he hesitated. Should he go back to his hiding place and try to climb the fence there, where Alpha Carter wouldn't look, or should he just run to the enforcers and beg them to help him? Alpha Carter was bound to notice him if he did that, but it was the easiest way to get out of here, and probably the fastest, too. It would also solve the problem of the fence, and Cooper wasn't sure he could climb it, especially not in the state he was in.

Front gate it was, then. He kept an eye on the front door, just in case someone saw him before he got to the gate.

He slammed against the gate and looked at the wide-eyed enforcers on the other side of it. "Help me, please."

He didn't have to say anything else.

****

Michael knew the man at the gate was his mate from the scent. He rushed to him, but the gate separated them. He could see how black and blue his mate's skin was, though, and he hated it. It made him want to storm the house and make the people responsible for the bruises pay.

Michael noticed Justin getting ready to shift from the corner of his eye. "No! He's my mate!"

Everything stopped. Michael could feel everyone's gaze on his back as he got even closer to the gate and reached between the bars. "I'm Michael."

"And I fucking need to get out of here before they realize I'm gone."

Michael blinked. This wasn't what he'd expected, especially not with the many bruises on his mate's skin. "Of course." He turned to Pryderi. "Can you?"

Pryderi nodded. He disappeared and reappeared on the other side of the gate. He was already reaching for Michael's mate when the front door banged open.

"They're taking him!" someone yelled.

They had to get out of here. Michael looked at Sarah. "I know we were supposed to go in today—"

"We're going home. Pryderi!"

Michael could see the guns in the hands of the men streaming through the door. The first shot was loud, and luckily for them, widely inaccurate. That didn't mean they could linger, though.

Pryderi reappeared in the middle of their group, and everyone reached for him. Michael wanted to get to his mate, but now wasn't the time, so he focused on Pryderi, because the last thing they needed was the shimmering to go wrong because Michael was obsessing over his mate.

They reappeared in the shimmering room in the enforcers' wing, and Michael let go. He pushed people away, ignoring their grumbles, and reached his mate. The bruises were even more evident now that they were illuminated by artificial light, and Michael reached for him, stopping just before touching him. "Are you okay?" he asked.

He was terrified of startling his mate, of making him afraid of him. He couldn't know what had happened to him, but he had a pretty good idea, and he was going to make sure that Alpha Carter and whoever had helped him beat his mate to a pulp paid.

Michael's mate pushed a strand of long brown hair away from his face and looked around. "Where are we?"

"In Whitedell. In the enforcers' wing."

"We need to regroup," Sarah snapped. "Everyone, with me. Michael, take your mate to the infirmary. I want to talk to him about what's going on in that house as soon as he's feeling up to it."

"I'm feeling up to it right now, and you don't have to talk about me as if I'm not even in the room," Michael's mate told her.

Michael had to suppress a grin. No one talked to Sarah the way his mate just had.

She arched a brow. "Really? What's going on in that house, then?"

"The usual, and by the way, it took you guys a while to realize this. Alpha Carter's an asshole who likes to beat people, including his twenty-year-old third wife, even though she had a baby a month ago. He hasn't hit the baby yet, but I wouldn't be surprised if it happened sooner rather than later, especially with me gone. I was his favorite punching bag, and he's not going to be happy at not having me to take his frustration out on anymore."

Michael tightened his hands into fists. He was going to kill that guy.

"What else?" Sarah asked.

"Let's see. He doesn't let anyone leave the house, and by the house, I mean that we're not even allowed to be in the garden anymore. He wants to make sure no one tries to leave the pride. He also controls who marries who because he wants the pride to have babies. That's why he's always hated me. I'm gay, and no matter how much he wanted me to, I couldn't get it up for a woman. So he started using me as the pride slave instead."

"And no one tried to help you?" Michael asked.

His mate finally looked at him. "Not after a while. Not even my parents. They had to think of themselves and their safety, I guess, just like I did when I climbed out of my bedroom window. I know he's going to be angry and take it out on someone. But I couldn't stay there anymore." He straightened his shoulders. "I'm not sorry, not for thinking of myself for once."

"You shouldn't be sorry. You did the right thing," Sarah said. "All right. Everyone, follow me. Michael and Michael's mate, go to the infirmary and see if someone can help with those bruises. I'd like to talk to you again later for more details, but I'm pretty sure Michael is going to tear my head off soon if I don't allow him to take care of you."

Michael blushed. "I'm not going to do that."

Sarah's gaze went soft. "I know, but you're worried about him, as you should be. Go, you two. I need to talk to Emerson anyway. You know where to find us when you're done."

She turned toward the door, and Michael's mate yelled, "My name is Cooper!" after her.

She laughed.

Michael waited until the others were gone to look at Cooper. "Are you feeling up to walking to the infirmary? It's right next door, but I can carry you, or help you walk, or even go get a wheelchair if you'd rather not touch me."

Cooper's shoulders slumped. "God, I'm so fucking tired. And I can walk, but thanks." He peered at Michael, part of his face hidden by his hair. "So you're my mate."

Michael smiled. He couldn't help it. "Yeah. And you're my mate."

Cooper laughed. "Well, now that we're sure of that and everything, I'd like to see your healer. Not that he'll be able to do much for the bruises, but maybe he can give me some painkillers? I have some, but I'm not sure how effective they are."

The bag Cooper had been carrying ever since he'd appeared at the gate was painfully small. Michael didn't say anything about it, but he promised himself he'd give Cooper everything he could ever want or need. He'd make sure his mate would live the rest of his life as happy as he could be.

He gently took the bag away from Cooper's hand, slightly surprised when Cooper didn't try to stop him. "Come on. Like I said, the infirmary is next door. We have a doctor and Nix healers, so they'll be able to help you."

Cooper blinked and followed Michael. "I didn't know Nix could heal bruises."

"They can, partly. From what I know, it's harder than healing an open wound, but they can help speed up the process. Besides, you have at least a few cuts that I can see, and those they *can* help you with." Michael hesitated. He knew Sarah needed to talk to Cooper because they had to know more about what they'd face when they went back, but Cooper's health came first. "I can tell Sarah you're asleep if you'd rather not talk to her today."

Cooper shrugged and winced. "It's fine. Trust me. I've had to work with worse bruises and wounds. I'm tired, but I can talk to her. I might not regret leaving the house, but I don't want the people still living there to have to go through what I went through. Alpha Carter is going to be pissed, and he's going to take it out on them, so the sooner you guys can go in, the better it will be."

Fuck. Michael could see it would be easy to fall in love with his mate. Cooper was banged up, more blue and yellow than pink, with cuts that had barely started healing, yet he was still thinking about other people, people who hadn't helped him when he'd needed it. He was a good man, a better man than the other Green Hill pride members deserved.

And he was beautiful. Michael wouldn't have cared even if he hadn't been, but he couldn't help but notice it. Even with the bruises and the swollen cuts, he could see how gorgeous Cooper was. They were about the same height, but Cooper was slighter. He had big brown eyes that didn't hold even a hint of fear, to Michael's surprise, and his long straight hair looked silky. He appeared delicate, almost as if he'd break if Michael held him too tightly, but Michael already knew that wasn't true. Cooper had a spine of steel. He was stronger than he looked, and that was probably the only thing that had allowed him to pull through what had happened to him, to get free.

****

Cooper was putting up a brave front, or at least he hoped so, but he was terrified.

Everything was new. He was in a place he'd never been in, with people he didn't know, and he wouldn't be going back home. He didn't know what would happen to him, if his mate would want to get to know him or want him in his life. Cooper had a lot of questions, but he was afraid to ask them.

And he was in pain, which didn't help.

Michael put a hand on Cooper's back and gently guided him into the infirmary. The room was big, and Cooper could see smaller rooms through their open doors. One bed was occupied, but he didn't peek into the room.

A man came toward them. He was wearing a white coat, and Cooper inched closer to Michael. Whatever happened, Michael was his mate, and he trusted him. He'd keep him safe.

"Michael. Please tell me you weren't hurt again," the doctor said.

Cooper frowned. Did that mean his mate was hurt often? Or maybe that he'd been injured recently?

"I'm fine. Not even a bruise, I promise. But my mate needs help." Michael turned toward Cooper. "This is Cooper. Cooper, this is Jared. He's been the doctor for the Whitedell pride for close to twenty years, and he also takes care of the enforcers. He'll patch you up."

Cooper swallowed and looked at Jared. He didn't seem like a bad man, but Cooper had no way to know. "You trust him?" he asked, hoping his voice was soft enough that Jared wouldn't hear him.

He was pretty sure Jared *had* heard him anyway, but the doctor didn't say anything about it. He just kept on smiling and waited patiently.

"I trust him with my life, and that's literal some days," Michael said. "He won't hurt you. He knows what he's doing, and he's been dealing with situations like yours for a while."

"Michael can stay with us in the room if you'd rather not be alone with me," Jared said. "I'll have to ask one of my Nix colleagues to take a look at you and see if they can help with the bruises, but again, Michael can stay with you at all times."

Cooper nodded. He was relieved he wasn't being forced to do anything.

Jared smiled. "All right. Michael, why don't you and Cooper go into one of the empty rooms? I'll see who's free to help him heal, and we'll be right with you."

Cooper stuck close to his mate as they walked to one of the rooms. He let Michael go inside first, then peered in. The room was plain, with a simple bed with white sheets, two chairs, and a nightstand. The window let in the sunlight, and when Cooper got closer, he saw the garden outside was magnificent. The sight of flowers took his breath away, and tears prickled his eyes.

"Are you okay?" Michael asked softly, as if afraid to startle Cooper.

And maybe he was. They didn't know each other. Michael had no idea what Cooper's life until now had been.

Cooper nodded and dried his eyes. "I'm fine. It's just overwhelming."

"Why don't you sit on the bed? We can go outside later, maybe this afternoon." Michael sighed. "Unfortunately, you're going to have to talk to Emerson and Dominic, although Dominic might not mind if you wait a day or two."

Cooper sat on the bed, his legs aching with relief. "Who are Emerson and Dominic?"

"Dominic Nash is the Whitedell pride alpha. I'm a pride member, so I'd like to ask him if you can become one, too, if you want to. I don't want to assume anything, and I don't want you to think that I expect something from you in exchange for taking you away from Green Hill."

Cooper frowned and cocked his head. "You don't expect anything?"

"Of course not." Michael put Cooper's bag in one of the chairs and sat in the other one, the one closest to Cooper. "Rescuing you doesn't mean you owe me anything."

"That's not what I meant. I know I don't owe you anything. You were doing your job. But I thought you'd expect us to bond. I do."

Michael's eyes widened. "You go straight to the point, huh?"

Cooper shrugged and instantly regretted it when pain burned in his shoulders. "Of course I do. We're mates. That means we're going to bond." And Cooper wanted it to happen soon. He already knew he'd fall in love with Michael and that he'd spend the rest of his life with him. He didn't see a reason to wait, and being bonded would give him extra protection against Alpha Carter.

Cooper didn't fool himself into thinking that this was over. The enforcers would investigate Alpha Carter, but he doubted they'd be able to do much about him, not right away. He knew Alpha Carter was going to try to get him back. He hated losing pride members, and he'd take it as a personal offense.

Michael opened his mouth to answer, but a knock on the door interrupted them. Jared stepped in, followed by a blonde woman with pointed ears. "Cooper, this is Lilah. As you can see, she's a Nix, and if you're okay with it, she's going to help heal those cuts and the bruises."

Cooper nodded. "That's fine." He couldn't wait for the

pain to go away, or at least to diminish. He was so used to being in pain that he didn't mind having to feel some of it, but he was tired. *So tired.*

"Why don't you stretch out on the bed? I'm going to examine you while Lilah takes care of the cuts on your face."

Cooper couldn't remember if he'd ever been examined by a doctor this way. He doubted it. Alpha Carter's father hadn't been as nuts as his son, but he still hadn't liked the pride mingling with other people, be they human or paranormal creatures. For him, seeing a healer was okay only if you were dying, and his son was even worse. Alpha Carter was lucky his wife's delivery had gone well, because he hadn't allowed a midwife to be there. The women of the pride had taken care of her, and Cooper had cleaned up after it was over. He remembered all the blood and stuff.

He stared at Michael through the examination. Jared prodded and poked at him, checking his stomach while Lilah's hand shone over Cooper's forehead. Michael never stopped smiling. He also looked like he was in awe, as if he couldn't quite believe Cooper was there. It was a new emotion for Cooper to see on someone else, especially because it involved him.

"All right," Jared said when he was done. He stepped away and nodded at Lilah, who moved down Cooper's body. She'd healed his lip, too, while he'd been staring at Michael, and it felt great to be able to smile without being in pain.

Jared moved closer to Cooper's face. "There are no internal injuries, so that's good. Lilah is going to help with the bruises, but you're going to have to come back tomorrow for her to finish. I'd also like to do some x-rays and bloodwork if that's okay with you, but it can wait. I'm sure you have better things to do than to spend the day here. For today, you can go eat something and rest. You deserve it."

Cooper blinked. "You're not going to keep me here?"

"You don't need to stay. You're okay, albeit bruised and no doubt in pain, but Lilah is going to help with that."

Cooper smiled. "Thank you." He'd expected to be kept away from Michael, and he was over the moon that he wouldn't be.

Jared nodded before turning to Michael. "You're going to talk to Dominic?"

"Yeah, although maybe we'll wait a few days. Cooper needs to see Emerson today because Sarah wants to go back to Green Hill as soon as possible."

"Okay. Cooper needs to take it easy and stay in the mansion. I don't want him to go out there with the enforcers. I don't care how much his help is needed. He has to rest and heal."

Michael raised his hands. "Trust me, he's not going anywhere, and neither am I."

Cooper didn't much like that fact that they'd decided without asking him, but he was tired. Maybe it wasn't a problem having his mate doing that, not when it came to small decisions. Besides, he didn't want to go anywhere, but especially not back to Green Hill.

"I'm going to take you to my room first so you can wash up and rest for a bit before we go see Emerson," Michael said once they'd left the infirmary.

This house was large, and Cooper was already lost. He probably couldn't have left even if he'd wanted to. "Can we bond?" he asked.

Michael stopped walking. "Now?"

"Yes. Please. If you want to, that is."

Michael licked his lips. "You're in a hurry?"

Cooper shrugged, and this time, it didn't hurt. "Why wait? We're mates. I know we'll fall in love. We belong together."

Michael smiled. "And Alpha Carter won't be able to do anything if we're bonded."

"That, too, but it's not my main reason for wanting to bond."

"Oh, it's not mine either, but it's a bonus. I want you to be sure, though. You know as well as I do that there's no going back if we bond."

Cooper didn't *want* to go back. He knew he never would.

CHAPTER FOUR

So apparently, they were going to do this.

Michael wasn't sure Cooper had thought about the implications of bonding with him right now, though, so as they walked to his room, he knew he had to ask, to explain. "You know that no one is going to send you away, even if we don't bond."

Cooper shrugged. He looked better, with his skin back to a normal pale color only slightly tainted by fading yellow. "You can't know that."

"I can. You're in Whitedell. It's basically where the council was created. Several council members live here. And of course, Dominic will know what happened to you, so he'll make sure no one can hurt you again. You don't have to bond with me to make sure you have a place here."

"What if Alpha Carter comes around and asks that you give me back?"

"Knowing what I do of him, he probably will, but that doesn't mean Dominic will agree. You're an adult. You have every right to leave your birth pride and become a member of a new one, even if we don't take into account that abuse."

"He could kidnap me."

Michael stopped in the middle of the hallway, and Cooper stumbled against him. "Kidnap you? Is that something he'd do?" Michael's mind was already running with it, thinking of ways to keep Cooper safe. It *would* be easier to find him again if they were bonded, but was that a good reason to do it? Michael thought it was, but he didn't want

Cooper to regret rushing into things down the road, once he was safe.

Cooper crossed his arms over his chest and glared. "Look, if you don't want to bond with me—"

"That's not what I said. I do want it."

"Then why do you sound like you're trying to find a way around it?"

Michael sighed. This wasn't how he'd imagined things to be when he'd thought about being his mate. "I'm just used to seeing people take things slow, you know? Meet, date for a bit, fall in love, and then decide to bond."

"And you think that's the way everyone should do it? You want to wait and date?"

Cooper didn't pull punches. He said what he thought when he thought it, and it surprised Michael. Or maybe not. Cooper wouldn't have been able to do this while he still lived with Green Hill pride, but maybe doing it now meant he felt safe. That was a good thing. "I didn't say that, either. I *do* want to bond with you." Because as Cooper had said, why should they wait? They were mates, and Michael had yet to see a pair of mates who didn't bond. Some fought, some took a while to let the other close enough to fall in love, but they always did and bonded in the end. "But I want you to know you have other options."

Cooper frowned. "Other options?"

"Yes. I guess I don't want you to choose to bond with me just because you think you don't have an alternative."

Cooper's frown deepened. "Alternative?"

"Yes. I know I told you you could become a Whitedell pride member, and you can, but you can also leave if that's what you want. You can go to, I don't know, Florida, or California. You can find a new pride there, or even stay prideless. You can start a new life without Alpha Carter breathing down your neck. You can be who you want to be, and *what* you want to be. Find a job, whatever. The Whitedell pride and the council will help you with that, give you the money you need to start over, guide you through job applications or college if that's what you want."

"What about you? Where do *you* fit in that?"

Michael sucked in a breath. They were mates, yes, but he hadn't been sure that would mean as much as it might once Cooper realized he could choose what to do with his new life and who he wanted in it. "Well, I live here. I'm a pride member and an enforcer. My brother is here, too, and I don't want to leave him."

"Then I don't see why we're talking about this. You want to stay in Whitedell, so we'll stay."

"Yes, but, Cooper, I don't *have* to be in your life, not if you don't want me to. That's what I was trying to say. I know we're mates, but you haven't started to live yet. You could travel and see the world and come back in a few years when you're ready for more with me."

"But I am ready now."

Michael needed to stop second-guessing everything that came out of Cooper's mouth. He knew he was doing it because he was scared — what if they regretted bonding so fast? What if they wanted different things in life, at least right now? Could they bond, then spend years away from each other, doing whatever they wanted? Or would Cooper insist on sticking around and resenting Michael for cutting his wings when he'd just gotten them?

Cooper huffed and stepped forward, grabbing Michael's face with both his hands. They were at eye level, and Michael thought he could get lost in Cooper's warm brown eyes, even though he was looking at him like he was an idiot right now.

"Do I have your attention?" Cooper asked.

"Yes."

"Okay. I never had a lot of people in my life. My parents are still alive, but as terrified as they are of Alpha Carter, they never stood up for me. I had a few friends who moved away a while ago, and we used to play together as kids. They're only a few years older than me. And do you know what we always played?"

"No." And Michael wasn't sure where this was going, but he liked to listen to Cooper's voice.

"That one day, we'd meet our mates. Alpha Carter and his father don't care about that. They mix and match people so they have kids for the pride. But we wanted more. Meeting your mate is like a fairytale. He's the one person who will never hurt you, who will always be by your side, who will love you when no one else will."

"That's—"

"I know. It's unrealistic. But I'm done with reality, Michael. I've lived in it all my life, and I want more. I know I have options. You just told me I could want the moon and you'd somehow find a way to give it to me. But I don't want the moon. I want someone to love and be with me, and I don't care if it's in Florida or here in Whitedell. I'm sure that if I ever want to see the world, we can take a vacation and go for a week or two. But I want a home, something I've never really had. Not just a mate. I want a family, not to go to college." He shrugged. "I've never been to school. I'm good at gardening, though."

Michael smiled. He couldn't help it. "There's a big garden here, and I'm pretty sure I heard the Nix in charge of it lamenting the fact that it's too much work for him and he wants to spend more time with his mate."

Cooper smiled back, and he was even more gorgeous than when he scowled. "See? Everything is already falling into place. I know Alpha Carter is going to try to come after me, and I know I don't need to be bonded to you if he does.

But I *want* to be bonded to you. I want to start that new life you were talking about, and I want to start it with you."

Michael's heart felt swollen, like it might explode in his chest. He reached for Cooper and pulled him into his arms, and Cooper came, his soft smile shooting straight to the center of Michael's heart.

Michael could have this. He was about to have it. Cooper wanted him, and he didn't want to wait, and Michael was more than okay with that.

He pressed their lips together, and he could feel Cooper was still smiling. He was also hesitant, and Michael remembered that this was probably his first kiss. He was both glad and pissed about that. He hated that Alpha Carter had taken so much from his mate, but Michael had the rest of his life to make up for it, and he would. Cooper deserved the world and, like he'd said, the moon.

Michael would find a way to get it to him.

****

Someone cleared their throat behind Cooper, and Cooper wanted to tell them to fuck off. The fact that he could tell them that, that he wouldn't be beaten for it, was thrilling, but he changed his mind about it as soon as he opened his eyes and turned around.

The man standing in front of him was tall, way taller than he was, and he looked like he could fold Cooper in half and carry him in his pocket without breaking a sweat.

"Hey, Dom," Michael said, and Cooper realized that the brick wall was Dominic Nash—*Alpha* Dominic Nash.

Well, shit. Cooper was pretty sure the best way to meet the man you hoped would agree to be your new alpha wasn't while making out in a hallway with your mate then scowling at him because he'd interrupted. He didn't think Alpha

Nash was like Alpha Carter, but that didn't mean he'd take this kindly.

"This is Cooper?" Alpha Nash asked.

"Yeah, it's him. We were on our way to see you."

Alpha Nash smirked. "Somehow, I doubt that."

Michael's cheeks flushed, and he was adorable. His hair was red and his eyes green, and they were Cooper's new favorite colors. He also loved the freckles dotting Michael's nose and cheeks, and he wanted to kiss every single one of them.

He blinked. Okay, so maybe it wouldn't take him that long to fall for his mate.

Alpha Nash offered Cooper his hand, and Cooper stared at it. Did he expect Cooper to shake it? To *touch* him?

Alpha Nash chuckled and dropped his hand, and Cooper felt like an idiot. "That's fine. Not everyone likes shaking hands. So, Cooper. I already found out you're Michael's mate. Does that mean you'd like to stay with us here in Whitedell?"

Cooper bowed his head. "Yes, Alpha. I'd like to be able to stay. I'm good at housework and gardening, and I can help with that or with anything you need me to help with. I'm not expecting to stay here for free."

"That's good, but it doesn't mean you're going to pick up our dirty laundry. Michael will explain what you should and shouldn't do, but it's easy. Just do your part, help in the kitchen and to keep the communal areas clean and neat, and if you want to work in the garden, feel free to talk to our gardener. He'll be happy to find out he might finally get some help."

"Thank you, Alpha Nash." Cooper hadn't expected things to be that easy. Maybe he should have, since he was Michael's mate, but nothing had ever been easy in his life.

Alpha Nash grimaced. "Can you call me Dominic, please?

Or Dom? I'm only Alpha Nash when I work with the council. The pride members are family, so I'd rather you and the rest of them use my name."

Cooper nodded. Alpha Carter had never asked him that. Hell, he'd have probably knocked a few of Cooper's teeth out if Cooper had dared to call him by his name. "All right. Thank you, Dominic."

Alpha Nash—no, Dominic, Cooper wasn't going to make the man angry on his first day there—smiled. "Good. Now that you're officially a Whitedell pride member—"

"I am?" It was that easy?

"That's what you want, right?"

"Yes. Please."

"Then you are. I'll make sure you're registered with the council, but that's not going to be a problem. As I was saying, now that you're a pride member, you have your pick of bedrooms. Unless you want to share Michael's. It makes no difference to me or anyone, so take your time thinking about it. Michael can ask my PA where the closest empty room to his is, and we'll get you settled down." He wrinkled his nose. "I suppose you're going to want to go to the mall? From what I heard about your old alpha, he wasn't the generous kind."

Cooper snorted, and nothing happened. It amazed him. Could it really be that he wouldn't get knocked around anymore? That his skin wouldn't be stained with the blue and yellow of bruises ever again? It was hard to believe, but Cooper wanted to. He didn't want to live in fear anymore. It wasn't going to be easy but trying to relax was the first step.

Dominic grinned at him. "That's what I thought. Well, the council and the pride both have funds dedicated to people who, like you, escaped or were rescued from bad situations. Again, Michael can talk to Keenan and ask him about it. I'm sure Keenan will want to go shopping with you, but feel free to tell him no. The sooner you do it, the easier it will be for him to accept that you're not his new best friend. And if I can give you advice, stay as far as you can from Nysys. Once he gets his claws into you, he doesn't let go, and you don't want to find him standing by your bed at three in the morning because he feels lonely."

Cooper had no idea who those people were, but he nodded. He was going to have to ask Michael to give him a quick rundown of the people who lived there, who they were and what they did—and who he'd have to avoid. It was hard to believe everyone in the Whitedell pride would be as nice as Dominic and Michael, but Cooper wanted to give these people a chance.

"Do you need anything else?" Dominic asked.

Cooper had no idea how to answer that. He had a lot of questions, but they could all wait. "No."

Dominic's expression softened. Cooper wasn't sure why. "We're not going to kick you out, Cooper," Dominic said.

"I know." And Cooper hoped it was true. But even if it wasn't, if they told him to leave eventually, he'd survive. Nothing could be as bad as living with Alpha Carter, and Cooper was finally free. He could do anything and everything he wanted.

And he wanted to stay with Michael.

He had no way to know if Michael and the people he lived with were nice people, but he had to take a chance. He was ready to do it because *he* was making that decision for once. He had that freedom.

"I understand it's going to be hard for you to trust us in the beginning. I know enough of the situation to realize what you've lived through and how strong you are. And since you're now one of my pride members, I want you to take your time to relax and to get used to living here. Take two weeks, a month, or even more if you need it. I want you to be comfortable in this house and with the people you're going to share it with. And feel free to come to me or my beta if you need anything." Dominic's next smile was warm, and it made Cooper relax. "Welcome, Cooper."

Cooper smiled back. He couldn't have stopped it even if he'd wanted to. "Thank you." Dominic *was* a good man, and that was one of the reasons Cooper had to tell him about Alpha Carter. "He's going to try something. Alpha Carter, I mean."

"I expected that."

"I don't know what, but he's obsessed with keeping the pride members with him. He's afraid of the pride disappearing, and it would if people were allowed to move."

"Well, whatever he comes up with, you're safe here. He can't get to you."

Cooper doubted that. He knew Alpha Carter well enough to know the man would find a way to get to him, illegal or legal. He'd be sneaky about it. Alpha Carter might be an asshole, but that didn't mean he was stupid.

"Look, Cooper. What do you want?"

"I'm sorry?"

"What do you want? In life, right now, it doesn't matter. I just want to know what you want."

Cooper didn't know. He'd never let himself think about this. "I want to be free. I want to be with Michael. I want to garden and take care of flowers."

Dominic nodded. "Then I'll do what I can to make sure you get all of that. I know the situation with Alpha Carter is scary, and like you, I know he's going to try something, but you're not alone anymore. You have Michael, me, and the entire Whitedell pride behind you, and even though you don't know most of the members, it doesn't mean they won't help. We're a big family, and that means something."

Cooper now had a real family. It was almost too good to

be true.

****

Michael couldn't remember the last time he'd been this nervous. Maybe when he'd applied to work as an enforcer and he hadn't been sure he'd be accepted? Or when he'd started training and had realized he had a lot of work to do to be up for the job? Or when he'd met Sarah and the rest of the team when they'd first been assigned together?

He didn't know, but he was sure it hadn't been the same kind of nervous. This one was worse. It was personal, so the way he felt like he might not be enough cut deeper. What did he know about being a good mate? He knew how to deal with a boyfriend, but it wasn't the same thing.

He pushed open the door of his bedroom and stepped aside so that Cooper could walk in. "I know it's not much," he started, but Cooper shook his head.

"Are you kidding me? This is more than I've had in my entire life, Michael."

Michael tried to see the room through Cooper's eyes.

The bed was a king, and it was to the right, with the headboard against the wall. Michael had made it that morning, but it wasn't perfect, and he hoped Cooper didn't care. The door on the left of the bed led to a private bathroom with a shower that was big enough for both of them to wash together if they wanted to. There was a fireplace at the foot of the bed, separating the bed area from the small living room. It wasn't big, just a few armchairs, and a small couch, a coffee table, and of course, a TV. The wide windows gave onto the backyard, something Cooper would enjoy. There was a tiny balcony, barely big enough for a few chairs, but Michael liked to take his coffee out there in the morning during the summer.

"We can ask to move to a bigger room;" he said even though from Cooper's reaction, he didn't think they would.

Cooper glared. "Don't you dare. I love this place."

Michael grinned. "Thank God, because I so don't want to move." He rubbed the back of his neck. "So, I guess I can sleep on the couch for a bit. You can have the bed."

Cooper frowned. "Why wouldn't you sleep in the bed?"

"Because I don't want to crowd you. I might not know every detail of what happened to you in the past, but I do know that this place is new for you and that it can't be easy to get used to it."

Cooper came to stand in front of Michael. "I thought we'd already gone over this?"

He sounded annoyed, and it made Michael smile. He'd half expected Cooper to be quiet and shy, possibly afraid of everyone, including Michael. He was surprised that wasn't the case. He liked it, though. He realized Cooper was probably trying to hide his fear, and it was working because he didn't look afraid. That didn't mean Michael was going to push him, though.

"I know what we talked about, and I'm not saying no to bonding." If it made Cooper feel better and safer, then he didn't mind. He might have waited in a different situation, but Cooper wasn't wrong. Why should they wait when they already knew they were mates and they seemed to fit in easily enough? And if it gave Cooper the safety net he probably needed, Michael was all for it.

"Why do you want to sleep on the couch, then?"

"I told you, I don't want to crowd you."

Cooper put his hands on his hips. Michael would never tell him this, not when he looked pissed, but he was adorable. His hair needed a brush, and he no doubt wanted a shower, but Michael loved the spine that hid under a delicate appearance. "What if I *want* to be crowded, Michael?"

"You do?"

Cooper's shoulders slumped a bit. "I think so. I can't remember the last time someone hugged me or even touched me with something that wasn't anger. The past decade, the only times someone paid attention to me was to yell at me or beat me. So yes, maybe I want to be held while I sleep, to be touched with something other than anger and spite. Maybe I want you to kiss me again and never stop. And I don't want you to sleep on the couch. I'm ready to have sex with you. I'm ready to bond. I'm not going to run from the room screaming if you bump into me."

Michael swallowed. He put down Cooper's bag, something he should have done a while ago, and closed the door. "Okay, I can share the bed with you, and we can bond and do whatever you're ready for. I just need to know if Alpha Carter or anyone else touched you in a way they shouldn't have." He prayed the answer was no, but he needed to be sure.

Cooper blinked. "What do you mean? I told you they beat me, especially Alpha Carter."

"I know. I meant, did they abuse you sexually?" Michael was trained to ask that kind of question, damn it. He'd dealt with too many abused victims, but Cooper wasn't merely that—if he *was* that.

Cooper jerked back. He looked horrified. "No! Gosh, no. No one ever touched me that way. Alpha Carter is all about reproduction and stuff, and I'm pretty sure he thinks I can pass the gay gene or whatever through touch. He wouldn't risk it, and no one in the pride would risk making him angry by touching me or having any kind of interaction with me. Even my parents barely talked to me."

Michael relaxed. "That's great. Well, not the part about no one touching you, but that you weren't hurt."

"Oh, I was hurt plenty of times. Just not the way you

thought. Are we going to bond now?"

Michael might have been offended by Cooper's eagerness if he didn't know Cooper really wanted this. He wasn't doing it to be safe or to make sure he wouldn't be kicked out. He was doing it because he couldn't see himself without Michael now that they'd met. And to be honest, the same went for Michael. Cooper had snuck into his life and had settled down in just a few hours, and Michael couldn't imagine life without him already. "Why don't we sit down and talk?"

Cooper rolled his eyes. "What do you want to talk about?"

"Well, you said no one has touched you in a long time. Do you have any kind of experience?" Cooper sounded eager to get into bed, but Michael wanted to do this right. He'd never forgive himself if they rushed into it and he hurt Cooper, or if he made him uncomfortable. Sex could be fun, and it would definitely be hot with Cooper, but they didn't know each other yet, and Michael didn't want to do anything that could send Cooper running, no matter what Cooper seemed to think.

Cooper sighed. He flopped onto the couch. "Well, Alpha Carter tried to get me to have sex with a woman, but I couldn't. I've never liked them, not that way. They're all soft, and they feel wrong. So no, I've never had sex." He sat up. "But I watched porn. Not often, because it wasn't easy to find a way to do it, but I know what we're talking about. And I do stuff on my own, too. I might not have experience, but it doesn't mean I'm innocent or that you're going to hurt me. You won't. I'm never letting anyone hurt me ever again without saying anything, and that includes you."

Michael felt better. He'd known Cooper was strong, and he was glad to see that strength extended to being with him. He wouldn't back down if Michael did something he didn't want or liked, and that was what Michael had been looking for.

"So what are you afraid of? That I won't be good enough?" Cooper asked.

"Of course not."

"Because I told you, I've watched porn. I know we need lube and three fingers, maybe four because I'm probably going to be tight. I'll do my best, though. I'll make you come."

Michael shook his head. "I'm not worried about that, Cooper, and to be honest, it feels like you're trying too hard to show both me and yourself that you can do this. And you can. I can tell you want to. But I want you to be yourself, Cooper. Forget porn and whatever you're thinking about. I don't want a porn star. I want you."

****

Cooper hadn't been expecting this. He'd thought his mate—or any other man he'd eventually have sex with—would want him to know what he was doing. And he did, in theory. That was why he'd watched porn when he'd been able to. He'd even taken notes a few times, although it was nothing he couldn't remember. Lots of lube, lots of fingers, and lots of patience. That was also why he'd played with himself sometimes. He'd wanted to be ready when the time came, and he was.

But Michael wasn't reacting the way Cooper thought he would. He'd been ready to use the stuff he'd learned, and now Michael was asking him not to?

"But . . . what am I supposed to do if you don't want me to use that stuff?" he asked.

"Whatever you want." Michael reached for Cooper. He cupped one of Cooper's cheeks, and Cooper found himself leaning into him. "What do you want, Cooper?"

"You."

"And you have me. What about sex? What do you want? Because I'd like you to make love to me. I've been thinking about this since I smelled you the first time yesterday."

Cooper blinked. "You didn't even know what I looked like."

"So? I knew you were my mate. I knew that meant you'd be perfect for me. And I still think that and want that, Cooper. Unless you'd rather do something else."

Cooper frowned. "Are you sure it's because you want it, or are you afraid of hurting me or something?"

Michael rolled his eyes and kissed the tip of Cooper's nose.

That small gesture rocked Cooper to his core. He could do that now. He could kiss his mate, be open about the relationship they had, and not have to fear he'd be beaten for it. He could stop being careful. He could stop walking on eggshells all the time and being afraid.

"I'm sure I want this, Cooper," Michael murmured. "And it doesn't mean me making love to you is off the table forever. We can try that next time, or something else. I'm not putting any stops in what we can do together. But we have time to explore all of that. So? What do you say?"

Cooper smiled. How could he not? And since he could do whatever he wanted now, since he was free, he surged forward and kissed Michael.

It wasn't as perfect as he'd thought it would be. He moved too fast, and their noses butted together. Michael jerked back, rubbing his nose. Cooper bit his lower lip. Wondering if he'd messed everything up. "I'm sorry."

To his relief, Michael laughed. "Don't be. I'm fine."

"I hurt you."

Michael straightened. "It's nothing. I've been injured lots of times while on the job. This isn't going to dissuade me from getting you naked and in bed."

Cooper grinned. That was what he'd wanted to hear.

He grabbed the bottom of his t-shirt and pulled it up. His first instinct was to fold it and hide it—Alpha Carter had taken his clothes a few times to punish him—but he knew that wasn't going to happen here, so he dropped it to the floor before opening his jeans. They slid down his legs easily. He was glad most of the bruises were gone from his skin. He wouldn't have wanted Michael to see him like that, not when they were about to bond.

Cooper frowned. "We're going to bond, right? I mean, we've been talking about sex, but we haven't talked about bonding."

Michael blinked. Cooper was surprised to realize Michael was staring at his body. He'd never thought of himself as being attractive, not when it had been beaten into him that the only attractive thing in people was the ability to reproduce. But Michael was looking at him as if he liked what he was seeing, and it made Cooper feel oddly shy.

He licked his lips and shuffled toward the bed, still wearing his underwear and his socks. He tried covering his body with his arms, but Michael caught one of them and pulled him close again. "You're ashamed of your body?" he asked. His eyes blazed as if he already knew he wouldn't like the answer.

Cooper shrugged. "Not really. I'm just not used to this." He wasn't going to tell Michael what he'd been told again and again. He didn't want to ruin this moment, not any more than he probably already had.

Michael nodded. "Because you're beautiful. You'll always be beautiful to me, no matter what you think. I know words probably don't help you as much as I want them to, but they're true. I like what I'm seeing." He hesitated, then slid his hand down Cooper's arm to grab his.

Then he pressed Cooper's hand against his cock.

His *hard* cock, from what Cooper could feel through the thick fabric of his jeans. He shivered. The knowledge that he was the one responsible for that sent a thrill through him. He'd already known Alpha Carter was wrong, but this was tangible proof of that. "Why don't you strip?" he told Michael. "I might not have hands-on experience, but I'm pretty sure this will work best if we're naked." He gave Michael a cheeky grin, or what he hoped was one anyway, and hopped onto the bed.

He bounced, then spread his body out. This bed was much more comfortable than the one he'd had in Green Hill, and he couldn't wait to spend the night there, and all the nights that came after this one.

It was hard to believe that this was happening and that he'd never have to see Alpha Carter again or to go back to Green Hill. It was easier when he looked at Michael, though, and all the bad thoughts plaguing his mind fled it when Michael removed his clothes.

Michael was right. They *were* perfect for each other, or at least Cooper thought so. They had a similar height, and they were both trim, but that was where the similarities ended. Michael's hair was red *everywhere*, and his green eyes glinted as he came closer. Cooper might have thought he was the cat shifter between them because of the way he moved, so smoothly and silently, prowling more than walking. He was still hard, and his cock pointed at Cooper.

Cooper licked his lips. He wanted to explore Michael's body, to mark it as his, and he didn't know which he wanted more or where to start.

Michael crawled on top of Cooper and sat on his groin.

Cooper groaned. "This is incredible."

Michael wiggled his ass. "Ready to come already?"

"Yeah. I'm sorry."

"Nothing to be sorry about. This *is* your first time after all, and you've been sheltered until now. I don't mind if this is fast. I told you, we'll have all the time in the world to do this again and again, and to take our time." He traced a fingertip around Cooper's nipple.

It puckered up, and Cooper shivered again.

"To be honest, I want to find out how you feel inside of me pretty badly, and in more ways than just physically. I want to bond with you, Cooper."

That was more than fine with Cooper. He wasn't sure where to start, though, and it took him a second to remember. "Lube," he breathed out. He wasn't sure he could focus on anything that wasn't Michael sitting on top of him completely naked.

Michael grinned and raised his body. Cooper wanted it back on him. "Don't move," Michael warned him. He leaned sideways and opened the nightstand drawer. Cooper expected him to hand over the bottle of lube he took out, but when he tried to take it, Michael shook his head. "Nope. I told you not to move, didn't I? I meant it. Keep your hands to yourself."

Cooper wasn't sure that was going to be possible, but he placed them on Michael's thighs and waited. He had no idea what Michael would do next, and he couldn't wait to find out.

Michael gave him a stern look as he opened the lube. Cooper couldn't look away from it, and his eyes went wide when Michael squirted some lube on his fingers, then reached behind himself.

It was suddenly hard to breathe.

Cooper could tell by Michael's expression that he liked what he was doing. He wanted to participate in some way, though, and since Michael seemed to be focused on himself, he rubbed his hands up and down Michael's thighs. When Michael didn't protest, Cooper slid one of them to Michael's groin and wrapped his fingers around Michael's cock.

Michael jerked and glared, but Cooper could see he wasn't angry. "Didn't I tell you to stay still?"

Cooper grinned. "I am. I'm not moving, not anymore."

"Somehow, I don't believe it will last long."

He was right. As soon as Cooper saw Michael's arm was moving again, he slid his hand up and down Michael's cock. Michael shuddered, but he didn't tell Cooper to stop, so Cooper knew he was into it as much as he was.

Thank fuck.

Michael whined and moved his arms. His fingers shone with lube. Cooper was pretty sure he was still wide-eyed, and he suspected he'd stay that way for a while. Everything was so new and so *good*, and he wasn't used to it.

Michael reached behind him again. Cooper expected him to need more prep, but instead, slick fingers grabbed his cock. He jerked up, almost throwing Michael off. Michael laughed and hung on, so Cooper didn't feel too bad about it. He doubted he could feel bad about anything, not with Michael still touching him.

Michael tsked. "You need to stay still."

"That's impossible."

Michael's laughter was like a light in Cooper's life, and he wanted more of it, just not right now. Right now, he wanted to be inside Michael, to have Michael inside him, inside his head, forever. "I promise to stay still if you hurry up."

Michael's smile widened, but he didn't tease Cooper. Instead, he straightened Cooper's cock and raised himself. Cooper held his breath. He screwed his eyes shut when the head of his cock pressed against Michael. He expected this to be hard, to take some time considering how tight Michael had to be, but he slid inside his mate easily, so much that Cooper opened his eyes to make sure Michael wasn't in pain.

He didn't seem to be. He was biting his lower lip, and his eyes were closed, his cheeks flushed, but no expression of pain was visible.

Cooper reached for him and yanked him down. "You have to bite me. Now." He hated admitting it, but he *really* wasn't going to last long, not like this.

The last thing he saw before twin pricks of pain made him jerk was Michael's wicked smile. With Michael's face buried against his neck, Cooper closed his eyes and tried to relax. He wasn't very good at it, though, and he kept on moving his hips, pushing up into his mate, then out, again and again. He could feel their bond, but something was missing. He needed to end this, to bind them together so no one could ever pull them apart.

Cooper sank his fingers into Michael's soft hair and held his head in place as he finally bit him.

He'd never tasted anything as good as Michael's blood. It sank into him, and it made them one, and he loved it. He loved the bond when it flickered to life, telling him just how much Michael liked what was happening, what they were doing together.

He swallowed. "I can't —"

"Just come, Cooper. Come on. I want you to."

That was enough for Cooper. He didn't stop moving his hips as he surrendered, and he was vaguely aware of Michael jacking himself off over him. He forced his eyes open because he wanted to see Michael come, and even though the pleasure they were sharing through their bond made it challenging to think, he managed to gather his thoughts long enough to wrap his hand around Michael's. Michael jerked, and his cock pulsed as he came, painting Cooper's skin, making him smell of him, as if the mark on Cooper's neck wasn't proprietary enough.

But it was. Cooper was Michael's, and Michael was

Cooper's. Cooper's heart was so full it felt like it might burst, but he needed it intact because he wanted to have decades to spend with his mate—and he doubted that would be long enough anyway.

CHAPTER FIVE

Michael licked his paw, doing his best to look like he wasn't paying attention to what was happening around him. He was smiling inside, though. This might not have been his idea of a honeymoon, but he was enjoying himself anyway.

The team had been put off rotation again to give him and Cooper time together. It happened every time a member met their mate or bonded, and no one had said anything about it. Michael suspected that at least Sarah, Hunter, and Pryderi were ecstatic over it. It gave them more time to be with their better halves. Michael had suggested he and Cooper could go somewhere for a week, maybe to the beach since Cooper had never been, but Cooper had said no. He'd wanted to stick around the mansion to get to know the pride members, so that was what they'd done.

And what they were still doing. Today they'd decided to stick to the backyard and shift. Cooper had only been able to do that in his bedroom in the last decade or so, since Alpha Carter had refused to let him and most of the Green Hill pride out of the house, and it had been obvious Cooper had missed being able to run in the forest. Michael had let him go on his own because he'd been so eager and Michael's fox legs were shorter than Cooper's tiger ones, but he knew Cooper was close by again.

He could feel him in his mind, and that feeling still made him giddy. Of course, they hadn't been bonded long, just a few days, and he still woke up every day wondering if everything was real.

It was, as was the huge tiger stalking him from the edge of the trees.

Michael knew the moment Cooper decided to pounce. He was trained for this, and while Cooper was bigger than him, he managed to escape easily. Cooper looked around, puzzled, and Michael lolled his tongue out at him. Cooper roared and jumped forward.

This was fun. Michael hadn't thought about the fact that he and Cooper would be able to play together like this. He'd focused on their human sides, because that was how they'd bonded and how they were getting to know each other. But being in their animal forms told Michael just as much.

Cooper behaved like one of the pride kids in this form, and it made Michael realize just how much he'd missed growing up. Alpha Carter and his father had always had a tight grip on their pride, and Michael doubted Cooper or anyone else had been able to be kids or shift and play around in the garden the way he and Cooper were doing now. The thought made his heart squeeze. He was glad he could give his mate this, but he also wanted to go find Alpha Carter and beat the shit out of him. That man was a menace, and he shouldn't be allowed to *be* an alpha. The council was working on that, but they had to find an outsider who would take the man's place, and that wasn't easy. No one wanted to barge into a pride, especially one that had been as isolated as the Green Hill pride had been, and become their alpha from one day to the next. The pride probably wouldn't accept it, and that was the main problem.

Cooper's paw glided along Michael's side, and Michael realized he'd been distracted. He jumped out of reach and ran around the porch, wondering if he could wiggle his way under it and taunt Cooper from there. It probably wasn't a good idea, if anything so he wouldn't give the kids playing around them that idea. Their parents would be pissed if they hid there — pissed and terrified. Besides, Michael *wanted* Cooper to catch him. Just not right away.

He hid in a bush and waited. When Cooper cautiously walked past him, he grinned and threw himself out of the bush, landing on top of Cooper's back. Cooper reared back, but Michael knew what he was doing. He clung to his mate's fur with his teeth, tightening his paws around him. It was a weird position for a fox to be in, but he wasn't just a fox.

Cooper looked over his shoulder, a wicked gleam in his eyes.

Michael understood why when he let himself fall to the side and almost squished him. He let go and jumped away, and Cooper watched him, his stomach exposed, looking like a big kitty.

Michael shifted. "Damn, you're gorgeous." Cooper hadn't given him time to look at him when they'd first shifted. He'd been too impatient to play. But he *was* beautiful. His tiger was big, albeit not as big as some of the other tiger shifters Michael knew. His fur gleamed in the sun, and when Michael tentatively reached out to touch him, Cooper chuffed.

It was adorable. Michael had already heard that sound from the other tiger shifters he knew, but it had a different meaning when it came from his mate. He rubbed Cooper's stomach, digging his fingers into the fur. He knew tigers didn't purr, but it was obvious that Cooper liked what he was doing. He looked like an oversized cat right now, relaxed and boneless as he let Michael give him a rub down.

"Okay, that's both adorable and something I wish I'd never seen," Nysys said from behind Michael.

Michael looked over his shoulder without stopping his hand. "What?"

"Your balls are out. I can see them from behind." Nysys' eyes were screwed shut, and he'd even put a hand over his face, although with the fingers so far apart that Michael wondered if he was going to peek. Probably. This *was* Nysys, after all.

"We were playing, and I doubt it's the first time you've seen someone who's not your mate naked. You live with shifters."

"I'm aware of that. I just don't often get an eyeful of balls." He snickered. "That was funny."

Michael rolled his eyes. "Sure it was. Did you need anything, or did you come here to look at my balls?"

Cooper rolled to his side and showed Nysys his teeth. He growled softly, and Nysys raised his hands. "I'm not here to look at your mate's balls, just to tell Michael, and you, I guess, that two guys asked for you."

Michael frowned. "Two guys? Can you be more specific?"

"Not really, because I wasn't the one who talked to them. They're waiting for you in the living room."

Michael wondered who they were. They couldn't be dangerous, because they wouldn't have been allowed anywhere near the house if they were, never mind in the living room where the pride spent a lot of time. That didn't help him figure out who they were, though. "Do they want to see me, or Cooper?"

"I'm pretty sure they asked for Cooper. I was just told to come to get you as if I were nothing more than an errand boy."

"Please. We both know you'd have come even if they hadn't asked you. You want to know who they are and why they're here."

Nysys glared and crossed his arms over his chest. "Are you saying I'm a gossip?"

"Uh, yeah. Everyone knows you stick your nose in everyone's business."

Nysys huffed. "Fine. See if I do you any other favors in

the future." He turned and stalked away.

Michael grinned and yelled, "Love you!" after him.

Nysys flipped him the bird.

"He's kind of weird, isn't he?" Cooper asked.

Michael wrapped an arm around his mate's waist. "He is, but you'll get used to him. And even though he's that way, he's a good guy. He'd give you the shirt off his back if he thought you needed it. Of course, you probably wouldn't want it, since he wears stuff the colors of nightmares."

Cooper cocked his head. "I don't know. I liked the pink mesh shirt he was wearing the other day."

The thought of Cooper wearing that shirt had a conflicting effect on Michael. On the one hand, that shirt was just about the ugliest thing he'd ever seen. On the other, it was mesh, and having Cooper wear that would mean seeing a lot of his skin and his nipples. Maybe Michael could stand the ugliness for that.

"Who do you think is here to see me?" Cooper asked. The amusement was gone from his voice. He sounded worried now.

Michael hugged him tighter. "I don't know, but whoever it is, you don't need to worry. Neither the pride or myself is going to let anything happen to you. You're a Whitedell pride member now. That means something to us."

****

Cooper didn't know what to expect as he and Michael made their way to the living room. He hated that he was frightened, but he knew it would take him a while to get used to the idea that he wasn't a prisoner anymore and that he was safe. He knew what Michael had said was true—even if he didn't have his mate, he had the rest of the pride, and all of them had made it clear that they'd protect him, as had Michael's team. It was overwhelming, but a good kind of overwhelming. Cooper had never had this many people on his side, and it was weird.

They stopped in front of the living room, and Michael looked at Cooper. "Ready?"

"I don't know. Will I ever be? I have no idea who's there."

"Neither do I, but nothing will happen to you, even if it's Alpha Carter."

"There's no way it's him." Cooper might have moved in with the Whitedell pride only a few days ago, but he already knew they wouldn't have let Alpha Carter in, not when they knew what he'd done to Cooper.

"You're right, there's not. So whoever is there isn't going to try to hurt you. They wouldn't have been let in otherwise. We can take a moment, though, if you're still hesitant."

Cooper shook his head. He wanted to get this out of the way. He was curious because he didn't know many people outside of the pride, and he couldn't believe any of the ones he did would look for him.

But he was wrong because when Michael opened the door and let him in, Lenny and Scott were waiting for him.

He hadn't seen them in close to fifteen years. Lenny had left the Green Hill pride first. He'd become an enforcer, and while he'd come back when Alpha Carter had refused to let his sister divorce his nephew because she'd met her mate, Lenny hadn't lingered around. Scott had left soon after him, and Cooper had found himself alone. He hadn't been close to either of the men in front of him, but they'd been his allies in some ways, and he'd missed them.

And now they were in front of him. He wasn't sure what to do about that.

"Cooper?" Michael asked, his voice soft. He sounded like he was afraid Cooper was going to bolt, and Cooper shook his head.

"I'm fine. I just didn't expect this."

Lenny and Scott got up. "Cooper," Lenny said. "Wow, I wasn't sure it was true, but it is."

Cooper nodded. "It is. How did you find out?"

"Gossip. A team member told me some of the enforcers here in Whitedell had been sent to Green Hill and that one of them had come out of it with a mate. I hoped it was you, especially after I got a description from another team member, but I couldn't be sure. It's good to see you."

Cooper wasn't sure what to do. They hadn't been friends in a long time, and he was touched by the fact that both Lenny and Scott had cared enough to come running when they'd heard about him. Of course, he'd have appreciated it more if they'd come to help while he still lived in Green Hill, but he could understand why they hadn't. Not only had they had their new lives to deal with, and in Lenny's case, his job as an enforcer, but things hadn't been as bad back then. Alpha Carter hadn't locked them in the house, even though some of the pride members, Cooper included, had been kept inside pride territory.

But they were there now, and that was the important bit. Still, he crossed his arms over his chest and glared. "It's good to see you, too. It looks like life treated you well, unlike Alpha Carter did with me."

Scott paled. "I'm sorry. I should have tried to at least talk to you before I left."

"Yes, you should have. Life with the pride was hell after the two of you left. I know we weren't friends, but I liked you, and you left me alone. Alpha Carter locked me in the house and used me as a slave. He beat me regularly."

"He wasn't like that before," Lenny said. His voice wavered. "I wouldn't have left without Scott if he had been."

"No, he wasn't. But he became that way, and he hurt me. I was lucky Michael and his team were assigned to come to check on the pride. I'd still be there otherwise, and trust me, that's not something I would have wanted. I hate Alpha Carter, and I hate the house."

Michael startled Cooper when he wrapped an arm around his waist. Cooper smiled at him. He was grateful for his mate's presence. Even though Scott and Lenny wouldn't hit him, they brought up bad memories, and Cooper wasn't sure he was ready to deal with them.

Cooper cleared his throat. "What are you doing here, then?"

"We wanted to check on you," Scott said. "And now I see we also have to apologize. Life with the pride was hard for all of us, but you had it much worse than us."

Cooper didn't want to stay angry with them. They'd made a mistake, but if he was honest with himself, he'd probably have done the same thing. Hell, he *was* doing the same thing. He'd left the pride, and he wasn't doing anything to help the people he'd left behind. He knew the council was working on it, but was that enough? Could he personally do more? He didn't know, and he wasn't sure he wanted to try. He'd been treated like shit by most of the pride members, and he didn't want to have to think of Green Hill ever again. He needed to put as much distance as possible between himself and that place, and that meant letting go — of his fear, of his resentment, of his pain.

"You're right, I had it worse than you, and I don't want to think about it," he said.

Lenny nodded. "Of course you don't. We just wanted to check on you, but we can leave if you want us to."

"I don't."

Lenny blinked as if surprised, while Scott smiled, and said," I'd like us to try to be friends again if it's possible."

"I'd like to think it is."

"Yeah? I thought you might want us to go. I'm sure we

remind you of bad times."

Cooper snorted. "Pretty much everything reminds me of bad times. But I'm not in Green Hill anymore, and I'll work through things. Michael is helping."

Both Lenny and Scott looked at Michael, probably curious. Cooper wasn't sure what they'd heard about him exactly, and he could tell they wanted to ask.

He rolled his eyes. "Michael is my mate, and yes, we're bonded. I told you, he smelled me when he was assigned to check in on the pride, and he didn't leave until he got me." There was more to the situation than that, but Lenny and Scott didn't need to know, and Cooper was glad they didn't ask.

Michael cleared his throat. "Why don't the two of you stay for lunch? I'm sure you and Cooper want to catch up."

"That would be great," Scott agreed.

Cooper was all for it. His anger toward Scott and Lenny was already forgiven, and he was curious about their lives. It sounded like Lenny was still an enforcer, but what about Scott? What was his life like? Cooper wanted to know. He wanted to know what he could have, what his future might be like.

He knew he could take time to figure things out. Dominic had told him that, and no one had asked him anything about the future yet. He knew what he wanted, but it was hard to believe he could have it.

They headed to the kitchen to see what they could find in the fridge, but Nysys was already there, taking things out. Cooper wrinkled his nose when he saw pepperoni, cheese, broccoli, leftover pasta, and chili. He wasn't sure he wanted what Nysys was cooking, but he didn't have a choice, because Nysys shooed them out of the room.

"I'm cooking today!" he announced.

"I hope you have Pepto Bismol at home," Michael

murmured.

Nysys whacked him on the arm with a wooden spoon. "Stop bad-mouthing my cooking. You know I'm not that bad."

Cooper relaxed. It was moments like this that made him realize how different this pride was from his birth pride. No one was afraid to joke around and tease. They loved each other, even though they sometimes fought. No one would hurt anyone.

Cooper had found his place, and it was as different from his birth pride as the night was from the day.

****

"Lenny, are you still an enforcer?" Cooper asked. "And did you end up bonding with your mate?"

Michael stayed out of the conversation. He was there to keep Cooper company, to support him, but he wasn't Lenny and Scott's friend. Right now, he didn't even like them. They'd left Cooper behind, and that had subjected him to more than ten years of suffering, abuse, and hate. If Michael could tell them what he thought of them without upsetting Cooper, he would, but Cooper looked like he'd forgiven them, and since he was the one who'd been hurt, Michael would follow his lead.

"I did, and Scott met his mate when he moved to Gillham. We've both been with them for almost fifteen years," Lenny answered.

"So you both live in Gillham?"

"We're both members of the pack, yes. And we're both mated to Nix, believe it or not."

Cooper laughed. "I can believe it of Scott, but you're right, I have a hard time with you."

Lenny stuck his tongue out. "Not funny."

"I'm pretty sure that's what your mate said when he realized you two were going to be stuck together."

Michael relaxed. Scott and Lenny weren't his favorite people right now, but they made Cooper laugh, so he couldn't hate them. Besides, how could he know how he'd have reacted in their place? Their situation might not have been as bad as Cooper's, but Michael couldn't imagine Alpha Carter had ever been a nice guy. Scott and Lenny had fled when they'd been able to, and they'd never looked back. It was pretty much what Michael had done, too, although he hadn't left anyone behind. His mother had been as bad as his father, and he never wanted to see either of them again. His brother had already been in Whitedell, so Michael had just left, and he hadn't thought twice about it.

Okay, so maybe he *could* understand Scott and Lenny. He didn't like what they'd done—or rather, hadn't done—but he understood.

"What did Carter do after I left, Cooper?" Scott asked.

That took the laughter right out of Cooper. He looked down, and Michael took his hand, reminding him he was there and that nothing would happen to him. Cooper gave him a small smile. Michael wished he could do more, but he couldn't. This wasn't something he could help with beyond being there when Cooper needed him.

"He closed off the house," Cooper said.

"What do you mean?"

"You know he's always been obsessed with keeping the pride members in Green Hill and with having more members."

"That's why he wouldn't let Elizabeth go to her mate," Lenny said.

"It is. And that's why he locked us in after Scott left. He didn't care much about Scott since Scott is gay and wouldn't have had kids. That's why he used me as a slave instead of forcing me to marry one of the pride women. I wasn't allowed to leave the house, not even to be in the garden. I had to cook, do the laundry, every chore you can think of. I was beaten every day, sometimes more than once a day if Alpha Carter got angry for whatever reason, even if I didn't have anything to do with it."

"I'm sorry, Cooper. We both are. We should have realized things had gotten so bad."

Cooper shrugged. "How could you have? You never came back, and I doubt you talked to your families again, except maybe Elizabeth, but she's been a tribe member since she had the baby."

Michael had expected Cooper to break down, but he was surprised to feel that he was content. There was some anger, and some sadness and regret, but Michael had thought things would be much worse. He'd tried to shield Cooper from what was happening with the Green Hill pride and the decisions that were being made about it, but maybe he shouldn't have. Cooper was stronger than Michael had given him credit for.

He cleared his throat, getting the others' attention. "I thought you might want to know what the council is planning for the Green Hill pride."

Cooper frowned. "You know something?"

"Not much, since I'm not a council member, but enough. I'm sorry I didn't tell you. I didn't want to remind you of the past and what happened to you." He half expected Cooper to get angry, but the only things he could feel were curiosity, and yes, a bit of anxiousness, but nothing as bad as he'd thought.

"I'd like to know," Cooper said.

Michael nodded and squeezed his hand. "The council has been talking about either finding an outsider to take Alpha Carter's place or disbanding the pride."

Cooper gasped. No matter what had happened to him, what had been *done* to him, it was still the place where he'd been born and where he'd spent all his life up until now.

"They can disband the damn thing for all I care," Lenny said.

Scott seemed more hesitant. "I'm not sure the pride would accept an outsider as their alpha."

"They wouldn't," Cooper agreed. "But I doubt they'd want to see the pride disappear, either. If there's one thing Alpha Carter is good at, it's making everyone feel like the pride is the center of the world, like they *have* to keep it intact. An outsider might have a chance if he knows how to shift things to his advantage."

Michael nodded. "I'm sure the council will agree with you. As far as I know, that's the solution they're leaning toward. They don't want to have to displace so many families."

"Do they already have an idea of who they want to take Alpha Carter's place?"

"Not that I know of. It's not an easy task, so I don't think there are many volunteers." Michael certainly wouldn't be one. He'd never be considered, of course, but even if he had been, he wouldn't apply.

"Is it going to be someone with experience as an alpha?"

"Probably." There weren't many alphas without a pack, but they existed. The hard part would be to convince one of them to become an alpha again. There was usually a good reason why they'd stepped down.

"What about right now? What's happening in Green Hill?"

"Nothing. I know there's a team of enforcers keeping an eye on the house, but they're staying out of things."

"Even though he's probably beating his wife?"

There was the anger Michael had expected to feel earlier.

"I know it's hard to understand and to deal with, but yes. We can't barge into the house and arrest him. He'd have an easy time getting out if no one testifies against him, and he'd go back or have his beta take his place to show goodwill. We need to have proof of what he's been doing and to have a replacement in place already." Michael sighed. "This is one of the hardest parts of this job. Knowing something is happening but not being able to stop it or to help. But we can't act too soon, because things would be worse if we did."

Lenny nodded. "I totally get that."

Michael was glad when Scott brought up his mate and how he and Lenny were on the same enforcer team. Cooper visibly relaxed, more than he had since Michael had met him, at least when they were with other people.

This was what he'd needed, people he knew and trusted — because whatever had happened in the past with Lenny and Scott, Michael could feel Cooper trusted them. He was closer to them than to the people of the Whitedell pride, and it was understandable.

Michael was glad his mate had this. He wanted Cooper to feel at home, to start living his new life, a life in which he was free and didn't have to be afraid anymore. And he wanted to be happy with Cooper, the way he'd watched Benjamin, his brother, be happy with his mate for so long. He'd been jealous of their bond, of the obvious love they shared, and now he had a chance at having it.

It would take time for him and Cooper to settle into their relationship and in the new life they'd share, but Michael had never been afraid of having to wait. He was patient — he wouldn't be an enforcer and Hunter's best friend otherwise — and since he and Cooper were bonded, they had all the time in the world.

****

Cooper was happy. He hadn't expected to feel this way when he'd first seen Lenny and Scott in the living room, but he was glad he did. He'd thought they'd bring back bad memories, and they had, but they'd also brought back good ones. The three of them had grown up together—they weren't brothers, but they were close in age, with Scott and Lenny being the same age and Cooper being a few years younger. They hadn't had anyone else to play with since they hadn't been allowed to go to school. They'd grown apart over the years, but it almost felt like everything was okay between them now. Cooper couldn't tell if they'd be able to continue being friends and to get over the years, but he hoped so. He might hate Green Hill and everything it represented, but he didn't hate Scott and Lenny, and having them in his life tethered him, gave him a base on which to build the next chapter.

"This was tastier than I expected," Michael said. He managed to duck just in time to avoid Nysys' palm on the back of his head.

"Of course it was tasty. I cooked it," Nysys said.

"*That's* why I wasn't sure if we would all end up poisoned or not. I guess there's still time for that, though. It's probably a slow-acting poison."

Nysys pointed a finger in Michael's face. "Shut your mouth, or I *will* put something in your coffee."

Cooper smiled and got up. He hadn't helped to cook, but he could help with the cleaning. Everyone else was relaxing around the table, including Scott and Lenny, and it felt like family. It wasn't something Cooper was used to, and he needed a moment to himself in the empty kitchen.

He stacked some of the plates, smiled at Michael when he asked if he needed help, and shook his head. He kissed the top of Michael's head, his heart so full he wasn't used to it.

The kitchen was empty, thank God. Cooper put the plates onto the counter by the sink to rinse them before he could put them into the dishwasher. The door opened and closed, and he turned to see Nysys bringing in another stack of plates. "You didn't have to. I'd have come back to take them."

Nysys shrugged. "It's a lot of plates, and I don't mind."

"You cooked."

"So? I know the rule is whoever cooks doesn't clean up, but I don't mind, and there's always a lot of stuff to put away since there are so many of us."

"Thank you."

Nysys smiled. "What for? We're a family. We all have to do our part."

"You did more than your part today."

Nysys' smile widened. "That's because I'm such a perfect guy."

Cooper laughed. "You're right, you are." Nysys had been one of the first people in the pride to welcome him, and even though the Nix was strange, especially next to what Cooper was used to, Cooper liked him.

Nysys looked toward the garden and frowned. "Who's that?"

"Who's who?" Cooper put the plate he was holding in the dishwasher and went to look.

His stomach dropped. "How did he manage to get in pride territory?"

"What are you talking about? Who is it?"

"My old pride's beta."

And it was too late for Cooper and Nysys to call anyone, because Beta Boyd was already opening the back door and walking inside, his gaze fixed on Cooper. "I thought it would be harder to get to you."

"What are you doing here?"

Beta Boyd grabbed Cooper's arm and pulled him toward the door. "I came to get you back, to save you from these people."

Cooper blinked. "To save me? From what? I've never been happier. I certainly wasn't this happy while I was in Green Hill. I'm not going anywhere with you."

Beta Boyd reached behind his back, bringing out a gun he'd been hiding there. "I think you are." He cocked and aimed the gun toward Nysys, who didn't look afraid, but rather, angry. "Unless you want me to hurt your new friend?"

Cooper hesitated. He knew Nysys could shimmer away if Beta Boyd shot at him, but could he do it fast enough so he wouldn't be hurt? And even if he managed that, what would Beta Boyd do if he was confronted? He had a gun, and even faced with shifters and Nix, he might use it. Hell, he'd probably use it if that happened, and that wasn't something Cooper was ready to risk. "I'll come."

"What?" Nysys asked, his voice too loud for Cooper's taste. "You can't go. Who knows what this guy is going to do to you?"

Cooper was pretty sure Beta Boyd wouldn't do anything. He was here to take Cooper back to Green Hill and Alpha Carter. He was the one who would do the hurting. "It's okay. You'll know where to find me, Nysys."

"Cooper —"

Beta Boyd pointed his gun at Nysys' face. "Shut up, freak."

Cooper took that chance to act. He and Nysys hadn't cleaned up the stuff he'd used to cook yet, and that meant the cast-iron pan was still on the stove, empty and waiting for them to put it away. Cooper grabbed the handle and hauled it up. It was heavy, but not heavy enough that he couldn't use it to hit Beta Boyd on the back of the head.

He didn't make a sound. The gun fell on the floor, quickly followed by the beta. Cooper's stomach turned at the sight of blood, and he dropped the pan. It clanged on the floor, and before Cooper knew it, people were coming into the room, crying out and asking questions.

Michael rushed to Cooper's side, and Cooper leaned against him, burying his face against his mate's neck.

"Are you okay? What happened? I felt your fear and worry," Michael asked.

"I'm fine." Cooper looked at Beta Boyd. "He's not, though. That pan was heavy."

Cooper wasn't the only one worried and scared. He was bonded to Michael, and that meant he knew what his mate was feeling just like Michael knew about him. Michael was terrified. Cooper could imagine why, but he hated that his mate felt that way. He didn't want him to, and it felt like the fear he was experiencing was looping around and coming back through Michael's emotions. "I'm okay," he said, hoping to reassure Michael.

Michael nodded, but he didn't let go of Cooper, and Cooper was grateful. He needed the support right now, the comfort.

"That's Beta Boyd," Lenny said. He crouched beside the beta and had to avoid the kick Nysys directed at Beta Boyd's side. "What the fuck?"

Nysys' hand trembled when he pointed at Beta Boyd. "That asshole had the guts to come in here and try to kidnap Cooper. He threatened us with a gun."

"And how did he end up bloody on the floor, and unconscious?" Lenny asked. He checked Beta Boyd's pulse, and Cooper prayed he found one. He wasn't sorry about knocking the asshole out, but he didn't want to kill him.

"Cooper took that pan and hit him with it."

Lenny whistled. "That'd do it. He's out like a light."

Cooper relaxed. Beta Boyd wasn't dead. Cooper hadn't killed him.

"He needs to be taken to the council jail," Michael said. "And Dominic and Emerson should be called." He moved forward, but Nysys stopped him.

"Stay with Cooper. I'll shimmer his ass to jail."

"It's not your job."

"You're right, it's not, but you can't very well shimmer him, and you should stay with Cooper. He needs you, and someone else can go fetch Dominic and Emerson. I'll be right back."

He crouched next to Beta Boyd, grabbed his wrist, and they both disappeared.

"This isn't the way I thought things would go," Lenny said.

He probably hadn't meant to be funny, but it made Cooper smile. "I don't think it's the way Beta Boyd thought things would go, either."

Lenny grinned. "You defended yourself. I bet he wasn't expecting that."

That much was true. Cooper had only tried to defend himself a few times, but since it had earned him worse punishments, he'd stopped. It felt good and empowering to be able to do it again and to see it succeed.

"Are you sure you're okay?" Michael asked.

He looked more shaken than Cooper felt. "I am. I'm not hurt, and while I was scared, it's over now."

"Good, because I don't know what I would have done if I'd lost you. I'm falling in love with you, Cooper, and I don't want you to be hurt, or worse."

Cooper wasn't sure what they could do to avoid that from happening, though. This was Alpha Carter's first step. What would the next one be?

CHAPTER SIX

"And when will you come back?"

Michael didn't know how to answer that question. "I don't know, Cooper. It depends on how fast the mission goes, on what the situation will be like when we get there." He kissed Cooper's temple. "I wish I didn't have to go."

Cooper rolled on his stomach and inched closer again, his face only inches from Michael's. His feet were bare, and he looked vulnerable, but Michael knew better than to believe that, especially after the way he'd knocked out his old beta the week before.

The man's presence there had been a mistake. He'd told the people at the gate that he was with Lenny and Scott and that he'd run late. They hadn't thought to check since he knew their names, and they'd let him in.

"You know you have to go," Cooper pointed out.

Michael sighed. "I could ask Emerson for another week."

"You could, but you won't. Your team needs you. *People* need you. You'll do more good out there than here with me."

Michael knew that. It didn't mean he wanted to go, especially with Alpha Carter still firmly at the head of the Green Hill pride. So far, the council hadn't managed to find a replacement, and if they didn't in the next month, they'd dissolve the pride. They were trying to avoid it, though. It was never easy, especially when the pride had learned to rely only on itself.

Cooper poked Michael's cheek. "What are you worried

about? You love your job."

"Of course I do. I just thought I'd have more time with you."

"That's not why you're worried, though. I can feel it, remember?"

Michael smiled. "That's one downside of bonding I hadn't thought of." But he wouldn't go back even if he could. He loved being bonded to Cooper. He loved Cooper, period.

Cooper stuck his tongue out. "You're just pissed that you can't get away with hiding stuff from me."

"Maybe. Just think of how hard it's going to be if I organize a surprise party for your birthday."

"As if I'd need to know what you're feeling for the surprise to be ruined. You know Nysys would tell me within sixty seconds of finding out."

Michael pulled on a strand of Cooper's hair. "True."

Cooper peered at Michael, and Michael felt like he saw right through him. He probably did. Cooper was good at reading whatever he got from Michael through their bond. "What's going on, Michael? Really?"

"I'm just worried about not being here if you need me."

"Ah. Alpha Carter?"

"Yeah. He hasn't made a second attempt at getting you back yet." When the enforcers had gone to him to ask why his beta had been in Whitedell trying to kidnap Cooper, he'd said that he didn't know anything about it and that his beta hadn't talked to him and had acted on his own. It was a crock of bullshit, but they didn't have proof, since the beta had refused to talk. That meant Carter was still in Green Hill, still the alpha, and Michael didn't like the thought of leaving his mate vulnerable to him.

"I'll stay here if it makes you feel better. Inside the house," Cooper suggested.

Michael knew how much that meant to him. He'd spent

time outside in the garden every day since he'd arrived in Whitedell. He loved being in the garden and taking care of the plants, and he'd start working there when Michael went back on his first mission. Cooper was free, and he was taking advantage of it. The fact that he would be ready to stay inside to make Michael feel better touched Michael.

"I don't want you to become a prisoner here, too. I'm just worried."

Cooper nodded. "So am I. But as you saw last week, I can defend myself, and if it makes you feel better, I can ask someone to be with me when I'm in the garden. I'm sure Nysys won't mind as long as I let him bring his phone or whatever he needs to pass the time."

"It *would* make me feel better."

Cooper's smile was gorgeous and went straight to Michael's cock. Michael buried his hands into his mate's hair and pulled him closer, kissing him.

His phone vibrated just as things were getting interesting. He was tempted to ignore it since his team wasn't on the rotation yet, but he knew better.

He groaned and let go of Cooper, who snuggled against his side and kissed his chest. He was glad he hadn't ignored it when he saw that Dominic had texted him.

I need you and Cooper to come to my office ASAP.

Michael didn't like the sound of that. "Dominic wants to see us."

Cooper looked up. "What for? Did something happen?"

"I don't know, but we'll find out soon enough. He wants us to go as soon as possible."

Cooper sighed. "Of course he does." He pushed himself up and tied his hair. "Let's go, then. The sooner we're done with him, the sooner we can come back here and finish what we started."

He was acting like he wasn't worried, but Michael knew better. He didn't bring it up, though. They were both wondering what this was about, and they didn't need to feel each other to know that, or to say it out loud.

Keenan waved them in when they got to his office, and Michael knew it was a sign that whatever had happened was serious. He suspected Alpha Carter was behind this. It was the only thing that made sense.

Dominic was behind his desk when they walked in, and he gestured at the chairs in front of him. "Sit down."

"What's going on?" Michael asked. He didn't want to sit down, but he knew better than to stay on his feet. He'd end up wearing a path in the carpet with his pacing.

Michael and Cooper obeyed, but before Dominic could tell them what was going on, Nysys shimmered right next to him, making him jump. Michael would have laughed if he hadn't been so worried.

"What the fuck did I just hear?" Nysys snapped.

"I don't know, Nysys. How about that I don't want you to shimmer into my office or inside the house in general because it's rude?" Dominic asked him.

"That asshole is trying to get Cooper back?"

Michael's stomach sank. He *knew* this had to do with Carter. He cleared his throat to get Nysys and Dominic's attention. "Can you explain it to us, too? You both seem to know, but Cooper and I don't."

Dominic sighed and raked a hand through his hair. It looked like he'd been doing that for a while already. "Alpha Carter filed an official complaint with the council."

Cooper snorted. "So now he likes the council, huh? What's the complaint about?"

"He says Michael kidnapped you. He wants Michael arrested, and you brought back to Green Hill, where you belong." Dominic raised his hands. "His words, not mine."

"Oh, I know." Cooper's eyes were wide, and Michael could feel the panic, even though he was hiding it pretty well. "What are you going to do? Will he drop this if I go back?"

"You're not going anywhere," Michael told him.

"I don't want him to hurt you."

"He's not going to do anything to me because I didn't kidnap you. You asked us to take you away, remember? And we're bonded mates, so there's nothing that asshole can do. He might have filed a complaint, but that doesn't mean the council is going to take this seriously."

Dominic cleared his throat. "We *are* taking this seriously, but not in the way Alpha Carter wants us to. I spoke with a few of the other council members, and they agree with me. We'd like Cooper to confront Carter in a place controlled by us, just as you would if the only problem was the complaint. He won't think anything strange by it."

"And what are you planning?" Michael needed to know. He needed to be able to plan.

"We finally have someone to step in as Green Hill alpha. We're going to arrest Carter for what he's done to the pride and Cooper, and it will be easier and, hopefully, painless if we do that in one of our offices." He looked at Cooper. "Everyone here knows you're here because you want to, and Jared already handed in his findings from the day you got here. Everything, every single bruise and cut, is on file. You're not going anywhere, no matter what Carter seems to think. But if you feel up to it, I'd like you to confront him."

Michael knew Cooper's answer before he said it. He wasn't surprised. He'd realized how strong Cooper was the day they'd met.

"Of course I'll confront him. When is the meeting set?"

****

The last thing Cooper wanted to do was to have to face Alpha Carter. He wouldn't have agreed the week before. He didn't want to agree now. But he was stronger, and for the first time in his life, he had support. He had no doubt Michael would be there with him and would make sure Alpha Carter didn't come near him, and as Dominic had said, Alpha Carter wouldn't be able to do anything except yell at him—if he even got the chance to do that. Cooper was looking forward to having him arrested.

He sighed. "All right, but I'd like it to happen as soon as possible."

Dominic nodded. "That's what I thought you'd say. Carter filed his complaint a few days ago. I was told yesterday, and I made sure he was told to come back today. I'm sure that to him it will look like the council is catering to him and maybe afraid of him."

Cooper hoped that was true. He didn't want Alpha Carter to suspect what was going to happen to him. Things would go smoother if he came and was arrested. Cooper could too easily imagine what Alpha Carter would do if he was confronted in Green Hill. He might not like any of the people he'd left behind, but that didn't mean he wished them to be hurt, especially not the children.

"I don't know," Michael said. "Isn't this a bit *too* soon?"

"It's up to Cooper. We can ask him to come back tomorrow, or the day after. I doubt he wants to wait that long, though. Cooper?"

Cooper swallowed. Part of him wanted to wait so that he wouldn't have to see Alpha Carter again. The other part of him wanted to get in the man's face and kick his ass. Since he doubted he'd be allowed to do that, he'd be fine with watching the man get arrested and telling him he was never going back to Green Hill. He couldn't wait to see the expression on Alpha Carter's face when he realized he wouldn't be the alpha anymore and that the pride might disappear. "Today is fine." He licked his lips. "Do you think I could talk to the new alpha? The one the council decided to pick as a replacement?"

Dominic smiled. "I think that's a good idea. I'm sure he'll be happy to get some insights from you. No one wants to be thrust into that position without having an idea of what's going on and what they should be careful about. I can see if he's at the council offices right now or if he can come. I know he needs to fill out some paperwork."

Cooper wasn't sure he could do all that the same day, but he nodded. Maybe getting everything out of the way would help him focus on his new life. He didn't want to have to think about Alpha Carter and the Green Hill pride ever again. "That's okay, I guess."

Dominic got up. "Ready to head out? The meeting with Carter is in a few hours, so you can talk with Galbraith before that."

"Galbraith?"

"Alpha Galbraith Brennan. He'll take Carter's place."

Cooper had never heard of him, but then he'd never heard of a lot of people, not when he'd been stuck in Green Hill all his life. "I see." Might as well get everything out of the way today. Cooper wasn't looking forward to it, but it was better than wasting time, staying home and worrying.

Michael stuck to Cooper's side as they walked to the shimmering room. Cooper knew Michael wouldn't go anywhere and that he could lean on him. It was a reassuring thought, and it made him feel better. Michael was there to stay, whatever he heard during the meeting with Alpha Carter. Cooper hoped Alpha Carter wouldn't slander him, but he knew better. "Michael?" he made sure his voice was soft enough that only Michael hard him.

"Yeah?"

"Alpha Carter isn't a nice man. He's going to say . . .

things."

Michael snorted. "Trust me, I'd already realized he's not a nice man. And whatever he says, I won't believe. I know you. I know him. It's a no-brainer, Coop."

"Good." Cooper had known that, but it felt good to be reminded of it and have it confirmed.

A Nix enforcer was waiting for them when they got to the room. She nodded at them and extended her arms. She didn't speak, and it made Cooper uncomfortable, but what was waiting for him would be worse.

The building they shimmered into looked professional, with nicely-dressed people walking around, talking and having phone conversations. Cooper felt underdressed in his jeans and a long-sleeved t-shirt, but Dominic was dressed the same way, and he didn't seem to care, so Cooper tried not to focus on it. Besides, he was only meeting Alpha Carter, and the man didn't have a say in his life anymore.

"I texted Gal. He's waiting for us," Dominic said.

They were ushered into a small office where a tall man with short auburn hair was waiting. His blue eyes glittered when he offered Dominic his hand. "Council Member Nash."

Dominic snorted softly. "Dominic. Come on, Gal. Cooper and Michael don't care what you call me."

Gal's shoulders relaxed. "I wasn't sure." He smiled at Cooper. "I've heard you were a Green Hill pride member until recently?"

Cooper swallowed. "I was. It's not going to be easy for you to get them to trust you."

Gal shrugged. "I'm used to this kind of thing. It's not the first shifter group I've taken over."

Cooper blinked. "So, what—you go around taking over prides, then leave?"

"Pretty much, once I find someone who can take my place

and I'm sure the pride or whatever group I'm working with is ready. The last thing I want is for another asshole to take over. Most of the groups I work with have been through hell and back and have had abusive alphas when they were lucky. When they weren't, their alphas were outright monsters."

Cooper didn't want to think about what that meant. He already had enough on his mind.

They sat down around the table, and Gal looked at Cooper. Cooper didn't want to talk about Green Hill, but he forced himself to, explaining who Gal would have more problems with, who he thought would be relieved not to have Alpha Carter at their head anymore, and who might be a good alpha. He honestly wasn't sure any of the people he mentioned would accept the job, though. The entire pride had been scarred by Alpha Carter and his father, and it wouldn't be an easy thing to come back from. But Gal looked strong, and he knew how to deal with this kind of situation. Maybe he *could* save the Green Hill pride. Cooper would never go back, and he didn't want to see anyone from Green Hill ever again, but that didn't mean he wanted them to suffer and to have to leave their home.

Cooper wasn't sure how long they talked, but he felt more comfortable with Gal when Dominic cleared his throat and told him they needed to go.

Gal rose from his chair and closed the notebook he'd been taking notes in. "You're meeting Carter, right?"

Cooper nodded. "I am."

"He can't hurt you anymore. He's not your alpha any-more. He might not know it, but you do, and that gives you an advantage over him. Don't let him see you still fear him. He'll take control if you do. Just focus on Dominic and on your mate, and everything will be okay."

Cooper should probably have been offended by the fact

that Gal thought he was afraid of Alpha Carter, but he wasn't wrong. He *was* scared. He'd been terrified of Alpha Carter since he was a kid, and that wasn't an emotion that was easy to get over, not even now that he hadn't seen Alpha Carter in a week.

He'd do it, though. He had to, for himself and his future. For Michael.

"Ready?" Dominic asked.

Cooper doubted he'd ever be ready to face his childhood monster, the man who'd terrorized him up to last week, but he nodded. Ready or not, he was going to do this.

And he was going to come out of it stronger and in charge of his life.

****

Michael's first feeling when he walked into the room where Carter was waiting for them was hate. He wanted to grab the asshole and punch that smug smile right off his face. He was pretty sure Dominic would turn a blind eye if he did it, but this was Cooper's moment, and he wasn't going to step in unless his mate wanted him to.

He could dream about kicking Carter's teeth out, though.

"Alpha Carter," Dominic said.

Carter ignored him. "Cooper. Thank God you're all right."

Michael gritted his teeth. He stood behind Cooper while Cooper sat in the chair in front of his old alpha. He wanted to touch Cooper, to remind him he was there, but he didn't want to get Carter's attention. He wasn't sure the man would remember he'd been one of the enforcers who'd come to Green Hill. Carter's attention was on Cooper, and while Michael hated it, maybe it should stay that way, at least for now.

Cooper seemed to sit straighter with Michael there, and Michael sent his love through their bond. He wasn't sure it would work and that Cooper would feel it, but at least he'd tried to make his mate feel better and to remind him he was there. "I'm surprised you care."

Carter's gaze flashed with anger, but he wiped it off quickly. "Of course I care. You're one of my pride members. I care about all of you. We were worried when you got kidnapped, and we haven't stopped looking for you. Your parents miss you."

From what Michael knew about them, he doubted they did, but he kept his mouth shut.

Cooper snorted. "I'm sure they do. Everyone misses the official punching bag, don't they? Who took my place? Who are you beating daily now?"

Carter's gaze slid to Dominic, then back to Cooper. "No one, of course. What happened to you? What did they do to you?" he looked at Dominic again. "He was never like this. Is he traumatized?"

"Oh stop it," Cooper snapped.

"Cooper—"

"No. I'm not going to let you intimidate me, or whatever it is you're trying to do, into coming back. I'm never setting foot in Green Hill again."

Carter smiled. "But you're a pride member. Your place is with us, and since it's obvious you're not thinking straight, I'm sure Council Member Nash will agree with me that you need to be protected, even from yourself."

Michael was pretty sure Carter didn't remember him. Maybe he didn't even remember that Cooper had told him he'd smelled his mate. He wouldn't think he'd won otherwise.

Dominic cleared his throat. "In the case Cooper can't make a decision for himself, someone will have to make it for him, of course. It would be for the best."

Michael knew Dominic wasn't giving in, and from what he felt, so did Cooper.

Carter rose from his chair. "That's what I was thinking. I'm going to take Cooper home now. I expect the council to investigate and to find the people who did this. Cooper has always been fragile, as I'm sure you can see from his appearance. I'm surprised he isn't hurt, but then, some wounds aren't visible. Who knows what was done to him while he was in the hands of his kidnappers." He looked at Cooper. "Come on, now. I'm taking you home."

Cooper crossed his arms over his chest and glared. "You don't make decisions for me anymore."

"You heard the council member."

"Yeah, I did. But you know who would make decisions for me if I weren't able to make them for myself? My mate. The man I bonded with. You don't have any power over me, not anymore."

That stopped Carter in his tracks. "Your mate?"

Cooper tilted his head and smiled at Michael. "Yes, my mate. We bonded the day I left Green Hill, and as I'm sure you're aware, mates have precedence over alphas." He wiggled his fingers at Carter. "So goodbye, and I hope never to see you again. You're an abusive asshole who shouldn't be allowed to be anywhere *near* a position of power, let alone be a pride's alpha. And your father wasn't any better. You take the cake, though, especially in the past decade. Oh, and I hope they take your kids from you. All of them, especially the boys. They need to grow up with a real father, and a real *man.*"

Cooper knew how to push Carter's buttons, because the alpha—ex-alpha as it was—lunged over the table. He tried to grab Cooper's shirt, but Michael was faster. He took the back of Cooper's chair and dragged him back. Cooper didn't protest, didn't move, not even when Michael pushed himself into the space between him and Carter.

"I'm going to kill you, you fucking faggot!" Carter yelled.

The door slammed open, and two enforcers came running in. Michael stayed out of their way as they rushed Carter. He wanted to help, but he wasn't there as an enforcer. He was there as Cooper's mate, and Cooper was the only thing he needed to focus on. That meant he got to watch as Carter tried to punch one of the enforcers. The woman ducked while the other enforcer grabbed Carter's arm and pulled it back.

They had him neutralized in seconds. They didn't even break a sweat, and Michael had to force himself not to grin like an idiot.

"What the fuck are you doing? He's mine! You have no rights over him!" Carter yelled.

Cooper didn't look impressed. He got up, and Michael had to stop him from launching himself at Carter. "I belong to no one!" he yelled back.

This was getting bad, fast. Cooper should be able to tell Carter what he thought about him, but the last thing they needed was for him to get into a fight with the asshole.

"Carter, stop yelling. You're under arrest," Dominic growled.

Carter pointed a finger at Cooper. He'd stopped fighting the two enforcers, but Michael didn't trust him. "He lied. Whatever he told you, he lied. He's always been a sniveling little bitch. Looks like he found someone more powerful than me to snivel to, but trust me, he's going to stab you in the back as soon as he can."

Michael almost laughed. More powerful? Him? Of course, Carter didn't seem to have realized he was Cooper's mate yet, so he was trying to shift the blame of what he'd done on Cooper. That wasn't going to work.

Dominic went to stand in front of Carter. "As I was saying, you're under arrest. You have abused your pride for years, and the council won't allow it to continue. We will put someone in your place until the pride can stand on its own and pick a new alpha who will be better than you." He paused. "That shouldn't be too hard."

Carter lunged forward, but the enforcers were holding him tight, and he didn't go far. "You have no right to take my pride from me."

Dominic leaned closer, and damn, Michael would have been afraid if he'd been on Carter's side of that glare. Dominic was a great guy, and a good alpha, but he could be damn scary when he wanted to. Michael supposed he was lucky never to have seen him this way. "It isn't *your* pride. Being an alpha doesn't mean owning your pride or your pride members. It means dedicating your life to making sure theirs is as good as it can be. It means protecting them from danger, even if it comes from inside the pride. You failed miserably, Carter. *You* were the danger, and I hope you haven't ruined the pride completely, because I wouldn't enjoy disbanding it, but I will if they can't work with their new alpha. As for you, you'll never go back to Green Hill. You're going to join your beta in the council jail, and if you're lucky, you might be released before you hit your one-hundred and fiftieth birthday." He turned around, effectively dismissing Carter.

Michael relaxed and reached for Cooper. His mate came easily, slotting into his arms the way Michael had always dreamed someone would.

"Everyone okay?" Dominic asked.

Cooper nodded. He was shaken—Michael could feel it—but he also looked relieved. "I'm glad this is over."

"It is. You're probably going to be called to testify, so you'll have to face him again, but you have the entire

Whitedell pride behind you now. We'll be right there to help you and give you whatever you need."

It warmed Michael's heart, even though he'd already been aware of that. Cooper had a family now, and this thing with Green Hill was behind him for the most part.

They could start looking forward instead of back.

****

Cooper didn't have any regret as he left the room—and Alpha Carter—behind. He kept his back straight and his chin high. He wasn't going to let that man intimidate him any longer, even though he was still yelling and insulting him. Cooper could hear him, but for once, the words just glided over his skin instead of digging in like needles.

"You okay?" Michael asked. He didn't try to coddle Cooper, and Cooper was glad. He felt stronger than ever, but also fragile. Seeing Alpha Carter had brought back a lot of memories he'd done his best to ignore over the past few weeks. He could remember all too well the pounding of fists, the sound of flesh against flesh and of bones breaking, the taste of blood. He'd never have to face it again, but he'd have to learn to deal with the memories and the pain they came with.

He cleared his throat. "I've been better."

"Do you need anything?"

"Not right now." He needed to go home and be able to stop thinking about this, but he didn't know if Dominic needed anything else from him. He was still in the room with Alpha Carter, and Cooper had no idea for how long.

"Come on. We can go grab something to drink," Michael said. He put his hand on Cooper's back and gently steered him along the hallway.

Cooper was relieved when the door of the room they'd

been in opened. He and Michael stopped and turned to face Dominic, who was watching the two enforcers who'd kicked Alpha Carter's ass—albeit not hard enough for Cooper's taste—as they were dragging him out of the room, kicking and screaming.

Cooper's heart raced. It was hard to believe it was over, even with the days he'd spent with the Whitedell pride. It would take him a while to get used to living there and to being a part of that family. The way they behaved with each other startled him every time he saw it, but he liked it.

And now, he was a part of it.

"Ready to go home?" Dominic asked when he reached them.

"We can? I thought I might have to answer questions."

Dominic shook his head. "You can do that at a later day. I'm sure you want to go home and relax. We have enough on him for now, and Gal is going straight to Green Hill from here. The pride is in good hands, and Carter won't leave this place anytime soon. You can take some time away from thinking about this."

"Thank you." Cooper had nightmares in which he was still in Green Hill, where he'd never met Michael, where Dominic didn't want him in his pride and kicked him out. Hearing that Dominic wanted him to relax and to be happy meant a lot.

The same enforcer who'd shimmered them to see Alpha Carter got them back to Whitedell. Cooper was tired, and he wondered if he could get away with dragging Michael back to their room and spend the rest of the day there. That was what they'd been planning anyway, since Michael was soon going to be sent out on a mission. Cooper hoped he wouldn't be gone for long and that he wouldn't be in danger, but he had to learn to deal with this, too. Everyone else did.

They left the shimmering room, and Cooper blinked at the number of people in the hallway. Most were on their feet, but some had sat down with their backs against the wall. Cooper recognized all of them—Nysys and Keenan, Michael's brother Benjamin and his mate, and a lot of others. It was almost as if the entire Whitedell pride was in the hallway, and Cooper looked around, wondering what had happened.

"Is everything okay?" he asked, leaning close to Michael.

"Yeah."

"Why is everyone here, then?"

"For you."

Cooper wasn't sure what to do with that statement, but he didn't have the time to think about it because Nysys noticed him. He screeched and rushed toward him, and Cooper flinched when Nysys flung himself into his arms. "Are you okay? What did that asshole do to you? Did they arrest him? I can go kick his ass in his cell, you know. You just have to say the word, and I will. I want him to pay for what he did to you, and preferably in blood."

Cooper looked at Michael over Nysys' shoulder. What was he supposed to do?

"Just go along with it," Michael mouthed—the traitor.

"Come on, Nys. Let the guy breathe," Benjamin said.

He was suddenly Cooper's favorite brother.

"I was worried," Nysys protested, but he let Cooper go.

Cooper took a step closer to Benjamin and stuck his tongue out at Michael. "What's going on?" he asked.

"We were all worried about you," Benjamin explained, but Cooper still didn't understand.

"Why?"

Benjamin patted Cooper's arm as if he were an idiot, and maybe he was because his eyes pricked with tears when

Benjamin explained. "We knew what you had to face be-cause Keenan told us as soon as you shimmered away. We were worried, because you're part of our family now, and we don't want you to get hurt. That's why we decided to hang around and wait with him. To see if you were okay." Benjamin smiled. "And you seem to be."

"I am. Alpha Carter was arrested, and a new alpha is being sent to Green Hill. The pride will be okay eventually, and I don't ever have to go back." Cooper got to stay in Whitedell, with Michael and all these people who apparently cared for him.

It was overwhelming, but Cooper's chest felt tight and warm.

"So, you two are expected for family dinner, but in the meantime, you can do whatever you want," Benjamin said. "I'd suggest getting as far away as possible from Nysys be-fore he decides to hug you to death again."

Cooper was on board with that. He grabbed Michael's hand and pulled him along the hallway, smiling and waving at the people who tried to talk to him. He *really* wasn't in the mood for this. He was surprised and pleased at the way eve-ryone seemed to care, but it was too much.

"They're not going to hunt you," Michael pointed out.

"Are you sure? Because you know Nysys better than I do."

"You're right. He'd probably hunt you down. We should run before he realizes we're gone."

So they did. Cooper laughed and let go of Michael's hand. He ran ahead. He could hear Michael chasing him, and it gave him a thrill. He was the bigger one when they were in their animal forms, but even his tiger liked when Michael came after them. They both knew how things would end, and they were more than okay with that.

Cooper needed the closeness to his mate to let go of the

thoughts plaguing his mind. He wanted to focus on Michael and their new life together.

He took his shirt off and dropped it to the floor. He didn't stop running, not even when Michael called out, "What the fuck, Cooper?"

Cooper checked that no one was coming before chucking his jeans, too. Then he shifted, not caring about his underwear and his socks exploding as his body grew and got furry. Michael laughed behind him, and Cooper turned to see him pick up the jeans he'd discarded. He was already holding Cooper's shirt, and he was smiling. "You couldn't have waited until we were back in our room? Or in the backyard?" He leaned down and unhooked the elastic band left by a sock around one of Cooper's legs.

Cooper licked his cheek. Michael jerked back and fell on his ass. "That's disgusting, Coop."

Cooper wanted to tell Michael he didn't usually mind when he used his tongue on him, but he couldn't talk, so he licked him again. Then he turned and ran away.

Michael's laughter followed him along the hallway. He didn't have to look back to know Michael was right behind him, and he didn't stop until he got to their room. Then he had to, because without hands, he couldn't open the door.

"See? You should have waited," Michael said as he opened.

Cooper shifted as soon as he was in their bedroom. "*This is why I did it. Well, one of the reasons.*"

Michael dropped Cooper's clothes on the floor. "I take everything back, then. You had the best idea."

Cooper was glad he agreed. He was even happier when his mate got naked, too.

CHAPTER SEVEN

"How are we getting there?" Cooper asked.

Michael was distracted by his mate's naked chest. Cooper was sporting several hickeys and marks, as well as the bite on his neck. It made Michael want to puff out his chest. He'd been the one who'd put them there, and their sight elicited a caveman reaction from him. The fact that his fox was smug about it, too, didn't help.

"Michael?" Cooper turned around and looked at him with an arched brow.

Michael blinked. "Sorry, what? I was distracted."

The smile Cooper gave him was wicked. "I noticed. I wonder what was distracting you?"

"You know what. What did you want to know?" Michael was tempted to throw Cooper back on the bed, but they were going to meet Lenny and Scott for dinner, and they had to leave soon. They didn't have time for another roll in the sheets, but they would later, and Michael was already looking forward to it.

He was always looking forward to spending time with Cooper, but he had to admit that naked time was some of the best. Those were the times when Cooper let go of his wariness and the shields he kept up, even with Michael. Michael wasn't hurt by that. They hadn't known each other long, and with Cooper's past, Michael wasn't surprised. He didn't want to rush Cooper and risk hurting him, and he didn't mind if it took him months to finally relax.

He was already much better than he'd been in the beginning, and Michael was enjoying getting to know him.

"Michael," Cooper whined.

Right. Cooper was asking Michael something. "Sorry. What did you want?"

"Who's taking us to Gillham? Because I don't think I want to shimmer with Nysys again."

"Why not?"

"The last time, he said we were going to the mall to buy me clothes."

Michael frowned. "You did come back with clothes."

"Yes, but he shimmered us to Italy. He said their sense of style was better or something like that. I didn't understand anything anyone said. I want to be sure we'll get to Gillham, Wyoming, and not Gillham, Pennsylvania."

Michael cocked his head. "There's a Gillham in Pennsylvania?"

Cooper huffed. "I have no idea. I was saying that to make you understand."

"Don't worry. Pryderi offered himself."

Cooper's shoulders relaxed. "Good. I like him."

"I think he likes you, too. I hope you and your friends won't mind, but he asked if he could stay with us, have dinner. I think he feels lonely."

"Lonely? What about the rest of your team? And of course he can have dinner with us. I told you, I like him. He's one of my favorites."

Michael pouted. "I thought *I* was your favorite?"

Cooper laughed. "After you, of course."

"Don't let Hunter find that out. He'll whine until you change your mind."

"That's a terrifying thought. Are you ready?"

"I am. You, on the other hand, are not. Or were you planning to go to the bar bare-chested? I can't say I don't enjoy the view, but I might become jealous if someone else does."

Cooper rolled his eyes and grabbed his shirt from the dresser. It was so easy to be with him that sometimes, Michael was surprised. He'd had boyfriends over the years, even serious relationships that had lasted for a few years, but he'd never felt this way. He knew part of it was the bond they shared. Being able to feel what Cooper felt was a big help in getting to know him and feeling close to him, but it was more than that.

Michael was in love with Cooper. He'd been in love with him pretty much since day one, and the emotion had only deepened.

He wanted everything with Cooper. And he would have it.

A knock on their bedroom door interrupted them. Cooper grinned and strode to the door, opening it and waving Pryderi in. "We're almost ready. Thanks for offering yourself to shimmer us there, Pryderi."

Pryderi's cheeks flushed. He'd left his hair loose, something he didn't often do. It shone under the lights, golden and soft-looking. He'd also dressed up—he was wearing a button-up shirt and a pair of black jeans, and if Michael wasn't mistaken, there was a hint of eyeliner around his eyes.

"You look nice," he told Pryderi, not in the least surprised when his cheeks became even pinker.

"Thank you."

"You didn't have to dress up, though. It's only dinner with friends."

Pryderi shrugged. "It was nice to get ready. I don't go out with friends a lot."

"I'm glad you're coming tonight, then. I feel we haven't spent enough time together lately."

Pryderi smiled. "That's because you've been spending time with your mate. I'm not complaining. I like to think you

and the others wouldn't mind if I found my mate and decided to spend time with him."

That made Michael think about what Hunter had told
him. Hunter thought Pryderi had met someone, probably in
Gillham. He hadn't named anyone, but Michael thought he
knew more than he'd said. He didn't mind Hunter keeping
secrets, especially when they weren't his, but the way Pryderi had volunteered made him wonder. Had Pryderi met
his mate? Was that why he looked so good and why he was
so eager to go to Gillham? Was it Nate, the bar owner? Michael remembered Hunter had teased Pryderi about that a
few weeks ago, and Pryderi's reaction had been telling.

It wasn't Michael's business, but he was curious.

"Ready," Cooper said. He'd put on a light jacket, and he
looked delectable.

"Should we go to the shimmering room?" Pryderi asked.

Since it was on the other side of the house, Michael could
do without it. "Nah. Shimmer us from here. It's okay."

"You don't have a blocker for Nysys?"

"So far, he hasn't tried to shimmer in here, but we'll in-
vest in one if we need it." And Michael would beat his skin-
ny ass. The bedroom he shared with Cooper was Cooper's
oasis of calm in the tempest that was the mansion even on
the best of days. He needed it. He needed a place where he
could relax and not be self-conscious of what he did and
said. If Nysys ruined that for him, Michael would make sure
he remembered his punishment.

They shimmered in the shimmering spot closest to the
bar. It wasn't cold, but Cooper still pressed his body against
Michael's side. Michael wrapped his arm around his mate's
shoulders and kissed his temple. He didn't miss the way
Pryderi looked at them, not jealous but wishful. Maybe he
had met his mate, and he wished he were with him right
now. "Are you meeting someone at the bar?" he asked

Pryderi.

"Oh, no. I'd just had enough of staying at the house. You know how it is. Everyone is busy with their stuff and their relationships, so I don't have a lot of company."

"And that includes me. I'm sorry."

"Don't be. I told you, I'm happy for you and Cooper, and we both know we'll be sent out soon enough. Spend all the time you have with your mate. It's what I'd do if I could."

"But you can't?"

"Can we talk about something else?"

Michael wanted to push, but Pryderi wasn't ready to talk. He knew he could come to Michael if he ever needed to, so Michael moved on with the conversation.

Lenny and Scott were already at the bar when they got there. Michael introduced Pryderi to them, but Pryderi seemed distracted, and he didn't participate a lot in the conversations. That was fine, since neither was Michael — Lenny and Scott were Cooper's friends more than his, and he still hadn't fully forgiven them for the fact that they'd left Cooper behind in Green Hill — but it made Michael even more curious. He observed Pryderi for a while before noticing he really did seem to be looking at Nate more often than what would be normal. He was trying not to let it show, but he wasn't doing a great job at it, even though he'd been trained for this kind of situation.

Michael leaned toward Pryderi. "Are you sure you're okay?" he asked.

"Of course I am."

"Because you've been staring at Nate an awful lot." Sasha wasn't working tonight, so he was probably with Hunter. That left Nate there on his own. He seemed to be okay with it, even though the way he moved was a bit stiff. Michael knew he had back problems.

Pryderi looked away from Nate. "I am not."

"Yep, you are. But it's fine if you don't want to talk to me. I could introduce the two of you, though. I know Nate."

Pryderi looked at Michael with wide eyes. "Please, no. Not yet. I just . . . I need some time. Okay?"

"Of course." Michael could tell something was wrong, but he couldn't help Pryderi if his friend didn't talk to him.

He'd be there for him when he was ready. Both him and Cooper would be.

You may also enjoy the following from eXtasy Books Inc:

Win
Catherine Lievens

Excerpt

The words danced in front of Win's eyes. He supposed that was a sign he wasn't sleeping enough. Or maybe it was the coffee? Whatever he'd told Beck and Roark, four coffees before lunchtime was a bit much, even for him. But he needed it to keep going, so he got up to get a fifth cup. There was no more space for his mug on the desk, and he had to pick up the four empty ones. He put them into the sink and went back to the desk, snatching his phone to call Kameron Rhett, one of the council members, to tell him he'd selected the assassins for the next jobs.

A knock on the door interrupted him before he could dial the number. He sighed, hoping it wasn't Roark with yet another problem they needed to solve. "Yes?" he called out.

The door opened, and of course, since Win had shitty luck, Graham walked in. Win almost groaned in dismay, but he managed to keep the sound in. It was especially easy because Graham was holding a plate with food that smelled divine, and it made Win's stomach growl.

Graham must have heard it—he smiled. "I knew you'd be hungry."

Win was, but he wasn't going to admit that. He didn't want to give Graham an inch. It would be all too easy to let him in if he did. Graham was already doing a good job burrowing under Win's skin as he was. "I'm not."

"Your stomach says otherwise." Graham came closer to the desk and tsked. "Where am I supposed to put this? Come on. Move those files."

"Graham—" Win didn't want to spend time alone with him, not any more than he already had. Graham hadn't asked him anything about them yet, but he was bound to sooner or later. Win knew he was lucky that for now, he hadn't. He wouldn't be lucky for much longer, not if he knew Graham—and he did, kind of.

He might stay away from his mate as much as he could, but that didn't mean he didn't look at him, that he didn't observe him. It made him feel like a creep most of the time, but it was all he could allow himself to have with Graham for now, and it had to be enough.

Graham was a good man. He cared for the assassins even knowing what they were and what they did. He'd fit right in when he'd arrived even though he didn't have a mate in the warehouse.

Not that he knew of, anyway.

Win realized he was going to have to talk to Graham sooner or later, and he anticipated that moment as much as he dreaded it. He wanted Graham in his life, and he'd have to tell him that if he asked, but he needed to focus on saving his family first. Once everyone was safe and he didn't have to worry about them more than usual, he'd allow himself to talk to Graham.

Of course, that would only work if Graham stayed away, something he didn't seem to be inclined to do.

Graham arched a brow. "Nope. Don't Graham me. You need to eat, and I have food. I know you didn't have breakfast, so don't even try to tell me you're not hungry again. Come on. Get those files off the desk before I plonk this plate on top of them. You know I'll do it."

Win did. He huffed and puffed as he stacked the files on one side of the desk. Graham wasn't wrong—he needed to eat. He didn't feel well, and he was hungry.

He knew he was neglecting himself and that it wouldn't end well for him if he weren't careful. He just needed to do more. He didn't know how, but he'd find a way, and that didn't include spending time with Graham and telling him they were mates or begging him to bond with Win.

"There." The plate clunked on the desk when Graham set it down. He leaned closer and wrinkled his nose at Win's cup. "What number is that?"

"What?"

"The coffee. Wait, let me guess? Number three?"

Win glared. "It's my fourth, and it's none of your business. Thank you for the meal, Graham. You can go now."

Graham ignored Win. He grabbed the mug instead and brought it to the sink, where he threw out its contents.

"Graham!" Win barked.

Graham didn't even look at him. He emptied the coffee pot into the sink, too, and turned the water on. He got a fork and a knife out of the drawer and took them over to Win's desk, depositing them next to the plate. Then he went back to the sink and washed the mugs.

Win couldn't look away from him. Graham was taking care of him even though he didn't know they were mates. There was no way he could, since he was human, although sometimes, Win wondered. Being human didn't mean he didn't feel anything. Humans felt the bond, too. It wasn't as strong for them, but there was no denying it. Was that the reason Graham kept coming back even though Win did his best to push him away?

Probably, and there was nothing Win could do about it. He couldn't change the fact that they were mates. He didn't want to. He wanted Graham in his life, just not right now. And he knew he owed it to Graham to talk to him and to tell him the truth, to explain what was going on, but he couldn't. It would take too much time from him, too much attention he needed to dedicate to finding the assholes who wanted to kill his family.

So he kept his mouth shut, at least when it came to talking. He did eat Graham's food, though. It was delicious, just like always.

And as he ate, he watched Graham.

Once Graham was done washing the mugs and the coffee machine, he wiped down the counter and the cupboards. He put everything away, and Win didn't miss that he didn't put on a new pot of coffee. It didn't matter. Win would make one as soon as Graham was gone.

"Oh, I didn't give you anything to drink. Sorry," Graham said. He opened the fridge, and even though he was at his desk, Win saw him wrinkle his nose. "Soda? Come on, Win. Don't you get enough caffeine in your coffee? Where's that herbal tea I gave you?"

Win had thrown it away, but he wasn't about to confess that, not to Graham. "I drank it."

Graham grabbed a bottle of water and closed the fridge. "All of it? Really?"

"Really."

"And you expect me to believe that?"

Win pressed his lips together. He couldn't smile. "I can't tell you what to believe or not, but it's the truth. Don't you have something better to do, Graham? Have you eaten, or did you come down here before eating?"

Graham put the bottle in front of Win. "I'll eat later. I have to cook a second time anyway, so don't worry about me."

Win looked down. "I'm not worried about you."

"Of course you're not. Drink that water, Win. The entire bottle. It'll do you better than another pot of coffee. And if you don't slow down on that, I'll take your grounds away."

Win leaned back in his chair and crossed his arms over his chest. "You realize you can't order me around, right? I'm the boss here."

"Yeah, yeah." Graham straightened the pile of files on the edge of Win's desk. "Finish your dinner, Win."

"I can finish it as easily if you leave."

Graham smiled at Win, and Win fell in love with him a little bit more. "I'm not going anywhere, so stop trying to make me leave. I'll go once you're done eating."

Win knew he wouldn't get anything else out of Graham. Win was stubborn, but so was Graham, and especially when it came to Win. Win supposed it was the bond again.

He wasn't sure how he was going to deal with it if Graham continued to act like this. It was becoming harder and harder to resist him, and Win suspected that one day, he'd stop trying and give in.

ABOUT THE AUTHOR

Catherine lives in Italy, country of good food and hot men. She used to write fantasy as a child, but it was reading her first gay erotic romance novel that made her realize that that was what she really wanted to write.

After graduating from college in English language and translation, she divides her day between writing, reading, taking care of her son and reading some more.

You can find her on Facebook and Twitter or on her website: authorcatherinelievens.wordpress.com

Email: lievens.catherine@gmail.com

Newsletter: http://eepurl.com/c-uvKn